Dig into this bucketful of stories and y̶ ̶ ̶ ̶ ̶ ̶ ̶ ̶ ̶ ̶
who lives in a cupboard, a mischief-making rabbit, a dog that
saves a ship, a greedy boy who loses a tooth, a king who can
turn things into gold, and many other strange and exciting
people and animals.

No story has been put in the bucket without very careful
inspection by children's book specialist Pat Thomson. All the
stories are tried and tested favourites, and all by top children's
authors – Astrid Lindgren, Adèle Geras, James Reeves, Beverly
Cleary, Alison Uttley and many others.

You won't want to stop reading until you get right to the
bottom of the bucket!

PAT THOMSON is a well-known author and anthologist.
Additionally, she works as a lecturer and librarian in a teacher
training college – work which involves a constant search for
short stories which have both quality and child-appeal. She is
also an Honorary Vice-President of the Federation of Children's
Book Groups. She is married with two grown-up children and
lives in Northamptonshire.

A BUCKETFUL
of Stories for Six Year Olds

COLLECTED BY PAT THOMSON

Illustrated by Mark Southgate

CORGI BOOKS

A BUCKETFUL OF STORIES FOR SIX YEAR OLDS
A CORGI BOOK : 0 552 52757 2

First published in Great Britain by Doubleday,
a division of Transworld Publishers Ltd

PRINTING HISTORY
Doubleday edition published 1991
Corgi edition published 1992
Corgi edition reprinted 1993 (three times),
1994 (twice), 1995, 1996, 1997, 1998

Collection copyright © 1991 by Pat Thomson
Illustrations copyright © 1991 by Mark Southgate

Corgi Books are published by Transworld Publishers Ltd,
61–63 Uxbridge Road, London W5 5SA,
in Australia by Transworld Publishers (Australia) Pty Ltd,
15–25 Helles Avenue, Moorebank, NSW 2170
and in New Zealand by Transworld Publishers (NZ) Ltd,
3 William Pickering Drive, Albany, Auckland.

Printed and bound in Great Britain by
Cox & Wyman Ltd, Reading, Berkshire.

Acknowledgements

The editor and publisher are grateful for permission to include the following copyright material in this anthology.

Ruth Ainsworth, 'Cherry Pie' from *The Pirate Ship and Other Stories* (William Heinemann Ltd), collection © Ruth Ainsworth, 1980. Used by permission of Octopus Publishing Group Library.

Simone Chamoud, 'The Three Hunters', reprinted from *Clever Clever Clever: Folk Tales from Many Lands*, selected by Jeanne B Hardendorf (Macdonald 1970). Copyright Simone Chamoud, 1933. First published by J.B. Lippincott.

Jean Chapman, 'The Nightingale' from *Capturing the Golden Bird: The Young Hans Andersen* (1987). Used by permission of Hodder & Stoughton Australia.

Beverly Cleary, 'Ramona the Brave' ('Mr Quimby's Spunky Gal'), chapter 9 from *Ramona the Brave* (Hamish Hamilton Children's Books, 1975), © Beverly Cleary, 1975. Used by permission of the publisher.

Adèle Geras, 'A Zebra for Helen' from *Apricots at Midnight* (Hamish Hamilton Children's Books, 1977). © 1977, Adèle Geras. Used by permission of Laura Cecil, Literary Agent.

David L. Harrison, 'The Little Boy's Secret' from *The Book of Giant Stories* (Jonathan Cape Ltd). Used by permission of the publisher and author.

Margaret Joy, 'Croup, the Sea-Dog' from *The Little Lighthouse Keeper* (Viking Kestrel, 1988). Copyright © Margaret Joy, 1988. Used by permission of Penguin Books Ltd.

Astrid Lindgren, 'Nursemaids' from *Happy Days at Bullerby* (Methuen Children's Books). Used by permission of Octopus Publishing Group Library.

Ruth Manning-Sanders, 'Knurremure' from *A Book of Dwarfs*. © 1963 by Ruth Manning-Sanders. Used by permission of David Higham Associates Ltd.

CONTENTS

A BUCKETFUL OF STORIES
FOR SIX YEAR OLDS

The Little Boy's Secret

One day a little boy left school early because he had a secret to tell his mother. He was in a hurry to get home, so he took a short cut through some woods where three terrible giants lived. He hadn't gone far before he met one of them standing in the path.

When the giant saw the little boy, he put his hands on his hips and roared, 'What are you doing here, boy? Don't you know whose woods these are?'

'I'm on my way home,' answered the little boy. 'I have a secret to tell my mother.'

1

That made the giant furious. 'Secret?' he bellowed. 'What secret?'

'I can't tell you,' said the little boy, 'or it wouldn't be a secret any more.'

'Then I'm taking you to our castle!' said the giant. Stooping down, he picked up the little boy and popped him into his shirt pocket.

Before long the first giant met a second giant who was twice as big, three times as ugly, and four times as fierce.

'What's that in your pocket?' he asked the first giant.

'A boy,' he answered. 'Says he has a secret that he won't tell us.'

When the second giant heard that, he laughed a wicked laugh. 'Won't tell us, eh?' he chuckled. 'Well, we'll just see about that! To the castle with him!'

The giants thumped on down the path. In a short time they came to a huge stone castle beside a muddy river.

At the door they met the third giant, who was five times bigger, six times uglier, and seven times fiercer than the second giant.

'What's that in your pocket?' he asked the first giant.

'A boy,' he answered.

'A boy!' chuckled the third giant. He brought his huge eye close to the pocket and peered in.

'Says he has a secret he won't tell us,' said the first giant.

When the third giant heard that, he laughed a terrible laugh. 'Won't tell us, eh?' he asked. 'Well, we'll just see about that! On the table with him!'

The first giant took the little boy from his pocket and set him on the kitchen table. Then all three giants gathered round and peered down at him.

The little boy looked at the first giant. He looked at the second giant. He looked at the third giant.

They were truly enormous and dreadful to behold.

'Well?' said the first giant.

3

'We're waiting,' said the second giant.

'I'll count to three,' said the third giant. 'One . . . two . . .'

The little boy sighed a big sigh.

'Oh, all right,' he said. 'I suppose I can tell you. But if I do, you must promise to let me go.'

'We promise,' answered the giants. But they all winked sly winks at one another and crossed their fingers behind their backs because they didn't really mean to let him go at all.

The little boy turned to the first giant. 'Bend down,' he said. The giant leaned down and the little boy whispered into his ear.

When the giant heard the secret, he leaped up from the table. His knees shook. His tongue hung out. 'Oh, no!' he shouted. 'That's terrible!' And he dashed from the castle, ran deep into the woods,

and climbed to the top of a tall tree. He didn't come down for three days.

The second giant scowled at the little boy.

'What's wrong with him?' he asked.

'Never mind,' said the little boy. 'Just bend down.'

The giant leaned down and the little boy stood on tiptoe and whispered into his ear.

When the giant heard the secret, he leaped up so fast that he knocked his chair over. His eyes rolled. His ears twitched. 'Let me get away,' he roared. And he raced from the castle, ran over the hills and crawled into the deepest, darkest cave he could find.

The third giant frowned down at the little boy.

'What's wrong with them?' he asked.

'Never mind,' said the little boy. 'Just bend down.'

The giant leaned down and the little boy climbed on to a teacup and whispered into his ear.

When the giant heard the secret, he jumped up so fast that he ripped the seat of his trousers. His teeth chattered. His hair stood on end. 'Help!' he cried. 'Help!' And he dashed from the castle and dived head first into the muddy river.

The castle door had been left open, and since the giants had promised the little boy that he could go, he walked out and went home.

At last he was able to tell his mother his secret; but she didn't yell and run away. She just put him to bed and gave him some supper.

The next morning when the little boy woke up, he was covered from head to toe with bright red spots.

'Now I can tell *everybody* what my secret was,' he said with a smile. 'My secret was . . . I'M GETTING THE MEASLES!'

This story is by David L. Harrison.

Nursemaids

One day last summer, the pastor in the big village invited everyone in Bullerby to a large birthday party. Well, he didn't invite the children, but Mother and Father and Uncle Erik were invited — and all the other grown-ups, even Grandpa. Aunt Lisa felt badly, because she didn't think that she could go because of Kerstin, her little girl. Then Anna and I said we could look after her. We were going to be nursemaids when we grew up, so it would be a good thing if we started practising right away.

'But do you have to practise on my sister?' Olaf said.

He would have liked to look after Kerstin himself, but he had to milk the South Farm cows and feed the pigs and chickens while his mother and father were at the party. Britta would have liked to help too, but she was in bed with a terrible cold.

Aunt Lisa was very happy when we told her what we wanted to do, but Anna and I were even happier. I pinched Anna's arm and said, 'Won't it be fun?'

And Anna pinched me back and said, 'I wish they'd hurry and leave soon, so we could start.'

But it always takes a terribly long time for people to get ready for a party — except Grandpa. He was ready at six o'clock in the morning, although they weren't supposed to leave until ten. He was all dressed up in his black Sunday suit and his best white shirt.

As soon as Uncle Erik had hitched up the horses, Grandpa went to the North Farm wagon and sat down to wait. This was even before Aunt Greta had started to put on her party dress.

Aunt Lisa kept on giving us all sorts of instructions until the very last minute, and then Father and Uncle Nils and Uncle Erik smacked their horses, and they all drove off.

Aunt Lisa had said that we should let Kerstin be outdoors as much as possible, because she was the least trouble there. At noon she should have her lunch which was all ready to heat; after that, she should take a nap for a couple of hours.

'Won't that be fun!' Anna said.

'Yes,' I said. 'I'm sure I'm going to be a nursemaid when I grow up.'

'Me too,' said Anna. 'It's really easy to take care of children. All you have to do is remember to speak softly and kindly to them. Then they mind you. I read that in the newspaper the other day.'

'Yes, of course,' I said.

'But you know there are people who yell at their children,' Anna said. 'And

10

those children never mind their parents, and they grow up to be real little horrors. It said that in the paper.'

'Who would want to yell at such a sweet little thing?' I said, and tickled Kerstin's foot.

Kerstin sat on a blanket on the lawn and looked happy. She has a round little forehead, and her eyes are bright blue. In her mouth she has four teeth upstairs and four down, which look just like grains of rice when she laughs. The only thing she can say is 'hi, hi,' and she says that almost all the time. Perhaps she means different things every time, but you never know.

Sometimes Kerstin rides in a wooden cart.

'How about taking her for a ride?' Anna suggested.

So we did.

'Come here, Kerstin, dear,' Anna said and put her down in the cart. 'Now we are going to go for a little ride.'

She spoke very softly and kindly, just

11

the way you should to little children.

'There now, aren't you nice and comfy?' she said.

But Kerstin didn't think so at all. She started to stand straight up in the cart and jump up and down and say 'hi, hi,' but, of course, we couldn't let her do that.

'I think we'd better tie her down,' I said. So we did — with a heavy piece of cord. But then Kerstin started to howl so loudly you could hear it a mile away.

Olaf came running from the barn and said, 'What are you doing to my little sister?'

'Nothing, stupid,' I said. 'We are just speaking softly and kindly to her!'

'Well, that's all right,' Olaf said. 'But also you'd better let her do what she likes, so she won't cry.'

We thought Olaf should know how his sister should be taken care of, so we let Kerstin stand up in the cart and say 'hi, hi,' all she wanted. I would pull the cart while Anna ran along beside Kerstin to catch her every time she fell. Then we came to a deep ditch, and when Kerstin saw it, she climbed out of the cart.

'Let's see what she is going to do,' Anna said.

Well, she showed us all right! There's something odd about little children. You think that their legs are too short to run very fast, but that's where you're wrong. A little child can run as fast as a rabbit if he tries to. At least, Kerstin can. She said 'hi, hi,' and ran right down into the ditch before we had time to wink an eye. There she stumbled and fell on her head in the water.

It's true that Olaf had said we should let her do what she wanted to, and she wanted to lie in the ditch, but we still thought we'd better pull her out. She was sopping wet and yelling at the top of her voice. She scowled at us as if it had been our fault that she had fallen in. But we spoke softly and kindly to her and put her back in the cart. We pulled her home to

13

get some dry clothes, and she yelled the whole time. Olaf was furious when he saw how Kerstin looked.

'What do you think you're doing anyway?' he shouted. 'Did you try to drown her?'

Then Anna said that he should speak softly and kindly to us, because we were children too — except we were big ones, of course.

But Kerstin went over and threw her arms round Olaf's legs and cried and cried, so Anna and I felt just as if we *had* tried to drown her.

Olaf helped us find some clean clothes for Kerstin. Then he had to go down to the barn again.

We put Kerstin's best dress on, because Olaf hadn't been able to find any other. It was very pretty — in white with tiny little tucks and ruffles.

'You have to be very careful of this dress,' I said to Kerstin, but it was quite evident that she didn't understand what I said, because she ran right over to the stove and got a big soot-spot right in the middle of her dress. 'Hi, hi,' she said.

We brushed it off as well as we could, but it was impossible to get much of it off. Kerstin laughed when we brushed her. She probably thought that we were playing a game.

'It's twelve o'clock,' Anna said all of a sudden. 'It's time for Kerstin to have her lunch.'

We hurried to heat up her spinach in a saucepan on the stove. I took Kerstin on my lap, and Anna fed her. She ate very well and opened her mouth so nicely that Anna said, 'She really is an awfully nice little girl.'

Then Kerstin said 'hi, hi,' and hit the spoon down on the table. All the spinach flew into my eyes.

Anna laughed until she almost dropped the plate, and I got furious with her. Kerstin laughed too, but she probably didn't know why Anna was laughing. She must think that it's quite natural for people to have spinach between the eyes.

Then all of a sudden, when she didn't want to eat any more, she closed her mouth tight and hit the spoon on the table again and again so that more than half of her spinach got on her dress. We gave her some fruit juice to drink from a cup, and

16

more than half of that got on her dress
too.

After that, the beautiful dress wasn't
white any longer but green and red with
just a little bit of white in certain spots.

'There's one thing I'm happy about,'
Anna said, 'and that is that it's time for
Kerstin to take a nap now.'

'Yes, that's one thing I'm happy about
too,' I said.

And then we took off all of Kerstin's
clothes again and put on her pyjamas.
When we had finally finished, we were
worn out.

'We're the ones who need to take a nap,
not Kerstin,' I said to Anna.

But we put Kerstin in her cot and went out of the nursery and closed the door.

Then Kerstin started howling as loudly as she could. We tried to pretend that we didn't hear her, but she cried louder and louder until finally Anna stuck her head through the door and said, 'Be quiet, you naughty girl!'

Of course we knew that you should speak softly and kindly to little children, but sometimes you just can't. But what the paper said was probably right: that children become regular little horrors when you yell at them. At least Kerstin did. She cried louder than ever. Then we both went into her room.

She was happy as soon as she saw us and stood up in her cot; she jumped up and down and said 'hi, hi,' the whole time we were in there. And she stuck her little hand out between the bars and patted me. When I leaned over the cot, she laid her cheek against mine.

'She's awfully sweet, even if she *is* naughty,' I said.

Then Kerstin bit my cheek, so I had a mark for two days.

We laid her down in the cot and tried to tuck the blanket around her, but she kicked it off. When she had kicked it off ten times, we didn't pay any more attention to her. We just said, 'Sleep well now, dear,' very softly and kindly. Then we went out and closed the door. Right away she started howling again.

'Enough is enough,' Anna said. 'Let her yell!'

We sat down at the kitchen table and tried to talk, but we couldn't because Kerstin yelled louder and louder and louder. Sometimes she was quiet for a couple of seconds but that was only when she took a breath for the next howl.

'Perhaps she has an ache somewhere,' I said.

'Goodness, what if she has a stomach

ache,' Anna said. 'It could be appendicitis, or something.'

So we *ran* into Kerstin's room. She stood up in bed, and her eyes were filled with tears, but as soon as she saw us, she said 'hi, hi,' and started to jump up and down and laugh.

'That child hasn't a stomach ache or any other kind of ache,' Anna said. 'Come on, let's go!'

So we closed the door and sat down by the kitchen table again, listening to Kerstin howl louder and louder. Finally she was quiet.

'Oh, how wonderful,' I said. 'She has gone to sleep at last.'

Anna and I took out Olaf's Old Maid game and sat down and played Old Maid, and it was very nice.

'Babies should stay in bed all the time. Then, at least, you know where they are,' Anna said.

Then we heard a strange noise from the nursery. It sounded like a little happy mumble, the kind of sound that children make when they are doing something pleasant.

'No, now this is going too far,' I said. 'It can't be possible that she's *still* awake!'

We tiptoed up and peeped carefully through the keyhole. We could see Kerstin's cot, but we couldn't see Kerstin. Her cot was empty. We rushed into the nursery. And guess where Kerstin was?

She was sitting in the open fireplace that had been beautifully whitewashed for the summer. I mean it *had* been beautiful, before Kerstin got there. It wasn't exactly beautiful any longer, because Kerstin was sitting in the middle of it with a jar of shoe polish in her hand. She was black with shoe polish from head to toe.

She had shoe polish in her hair and shoe polish all over her face and shoe polish on her hands and on her pyjamas and on her feet, and all of the fireplace was decorated with shoe polish. Probably Uncle Nils had stood by the fireplace to polish his shoes before the party and then hadn't put the cover back on the jar.

'Hi, hi,' Kerstin said when she saw us.

'Did it say in the paper whether you could spank little children?' I said.

'I don't remember,' Anna said.

Then Kerstin stood up and ran towards Anna, and Anna yelled even louder than she did, *'Don't touch me, you naughty girl!'*

Kerstin did touch her. Anna grabbed her hands but still got shoe polish all over herself. Then I laughed just as hard at Anna as she had at me when I had got the spinach between my eyes.

'Aunt Lisa won't know her child when she sees her,' I said, when I had stopped laughing.

We didn't know how to wash off shoe polish, so we decided to ask Britta. Anna, who was already smeared, would stay and hold Kerstin while I went to ask her.

When I told Britta what Kerstin had done, she said, 'Well, you're a fine pair of nursemaids!' Then she blew her nose and turned towards the wall and said that she was ill and didn't know how you washed off shoe polish.

In the meantime Olaf had come from the barn, and he went absolutely wild when he saw Kerstin.

'Are you out of your minds?' he yelled. 'Have you painted her black?'

We tried to explain to him that it wasn't our fault. But Olaf was furious and said that there should be a law against people like us becoming nursemaids, and, in any case, we'd have to get another child to practise on.

But we all helped one another fill a tub with warm water. Then we carried it out on the lawn and led Kerstin out to it. When she walked across the floor, she left funny little black footprints.

We put her in the tub and scrubbed her thoroughly from top to toe. We washed her hair too. She got a little soap in her eyes, and then she yelled so loudly you could hear it all over Bullerby. Lars and

23

Pip came running and asked if we were slaughtering pigs.

'No,' Olaf said. 'It's just these two fine nursemaids who are practising.'

We couldn't get the shoe polish really off, and when we had finished scrubbing and drying Kerstin, she was a peculiar grey colour all over. But she was happy none the less. She ran around on the lawn, stark naked, and yelled 'hi, hi,' and laughed so you could see every tooth in her mouth. Olaf said, 'Isn't she a darling baby?'

We thought that the grey colour would probably wear off in time so the pink child who was underneath would show up again. It would be around Christmas time, Lars thought.

Afterwards Olaf put Kerstin to bed. She didn't say boo, just stuck her thumb in her mouth and went to sleep.

'That's the way to take care of children,' Olaf said. Then he went to feed the pigs.

Anna and I sat down on the kitchen steps to rest.

'Poor Aunt Lisa, who has it like this every day,' I said.

'Do you know what I think?' Anna said. 'I think all that in the paper was a lie, because it doesn't make any difference *how* you talk to little children. Whether you talk softly and kindly or yell at them, they still do exactly as they please.'

After that we were quiet a while.

'Anna, are you going to be a nursemaid when you grow up?' I said finally.

'Perhaps,' Anna said. But then she looked thoughtful and stared out over the barn roof and said, 'Well, I really don't know.'

This story is by Astrid Lindgren.

How Rabbit Stole the Fire

In the beginning there was no fire on Earth, and the world was cold.

The Sky People had fire. But they lived high up in the mountains, and guarded it from the animals.

'Who will steal the fire?' asked the animals, when the leaves began to fall and the cold winds blew.

The bison was strong. The wolf was cunning. The bear was brave. The wildcat was fierce. But Rabbit was leader of them all in mischief.

Rabbit made himself a wonderful head-dress. Each feather, every stitch he coated with pine resin.

'Here I go,' said Rabbit, putting on the wonderful headdress. And off he went to the village of the Sky People. As he went he sang a song. 'Oh, I am going to fetch the fire, to fetch the fire, to fetch the fire.' For that was what he was going to do.

'Here is Rabbit,' muttered the Sky People. 'He is a liar. He is a trickster. He is the chief mischief-maker. Do not trust him.'

'Hello, Sky People,' said Rabbit. 'I have come to teach you a new dance. Look at my dancing hat. It is a dance to bring the corn from the Earth. It is a dance to guide the fish to your nets.'

So spoke Rabbit the trickster. And with his words he soothed the Sky People. He charmed them. He flattered them. They forgot that he was a mischief-maker and welcomed him into their village.

'Rabbit shall lead us in the dance!'

So Rabbit led the dance! Round and round the fire danced Rabbit. And round and round behind him danced the Sky

People. Round and round danced Rabbit, wearing his wonderful headdress . . . and as he danced, he bent low to the fire, singing his dancing song. And the Sky People bent low also. Round and round danced Rabbit, and very low he bent . . .

Whoosh! The headdress was alight! And away raced Rabbit, out of the village and down the mountain.

'We have been tricked!' screamed the Sky People. 'Rabbit has stolen the fire!'

Rabbit ran and the Sky People followed.

They made a great rain. They made
thunder and lightning. They made sleet.
They made snow. But the wonderful
headdress with the resin-coated feathers
burned brightly.

Rabbit was soon tired. 'Squirrel! Take
the headdress,' he gasped.

Squirrel took the headdress and ran. As
she went, the heat made her tail curl up
and over her back. And so are squirrels to
this day.

Squirrel was soon tired. 'Crow! Take the headdress,' she chattered.

Crow took the headdress and flew. As he went, the smoke turned all his feathers black. And so are crows to this day.

Crow was soon tired. 'Racoon! Take the headdress,' he cawed.

Racoon took the headdress and ran. As she went, some ash burned rings around her tail and face. And so are racoons to this day.

Racoon was soon tired. 'Turkey! Take the headdress,' she panted.

Turkey took the headdress and ran. As he went, the fire burned all the feathers off his head and neck. And so are turkeys to this day.

But Turkey was not a fast runner, and the fire began to die.

'Set my tail alight,' said Deer. For in those days deer had long tails.

Deer took the fire on her tail, and ran so fast that she made a wind to fan the flames. Deer cried to the trees as she

30

passed, flicking her tail this way and that, 'Trees, hide the fire!'

The trees took the fire and hid it in their wood. But the fire had burned off most of Deer's tail. And so are deer to this day.

The Sky People returned to their village high in the mountains. Wood had hidden fire and they didn't know how to find it again. But Rabbit, leader of all mischief, knew. It was he who showed the animals how to find fire again by rubbing two sticks together. Now the animals have fire to warm the cold winters, and light to brighten the dark nights.

This story is a retelling of the traditional tale by Joanna Troughton

Author's Note

This story of rabbit and how he brought fire to the earth comes from the South East of the USA and is told by the Creek, the Hitchiti and the Koasati Indians. Stories of rabbit the trickster and wonder-worker are found in all the areas east of the Mississippi from Hudson Bay to the Gulf of Mexico.

31

A Zebra for Helen

A patchwork quilt story

Aunt Pinny sat at the foot of my bed, gently stroking a small patch of black-and-white striped material.

'Why are you stroking that?' I asked.

'Because it reminds me of Helen. She was my first real friend, and these stripes remind me of the day I first met her. Shall I tell you about it?'

'Yes, please,' I said, and pulled the quilt up round my shoulders.

'Helen comes into the story at the end, although, as you shall see, she's very important. It all began a few weeks before Christmas. I was six years old. My

mother was spending every spare moment cutting, stitching and stuffing soft
toys. They were not for me. They were to
be sold at the Christmas jumble sale in our
Church Hall, to raise money for a nearby
orphanage. I longed for some of them,
though. There were velvet rabbits,
elephants with silken ears, and a chicken
trimmed with real feathers. There was a
plush cat with huge, gold buttons for eyes
and a tiny felt mouth. There was even a
lion with real woollen strands standing
out round his head. I said to my mother:
"Why don't you ever make animals like
these for me?"

' "Because, child, I have our living to
earn. My dresses would never be finished
if I spent all my time on toys."

' "But you're spending all your time on
toys now," I muttered, near to tears.

'My mother put down the satin snake
she was sewing. "Darling, that's for char-
ity. And besides, you know Miss Snow.
It's very hard to say 'no' to such a lady!"

'That was true. Miss Snow, our Vicar's sister, was a solid mountain of a woman, tightly squeezed into grey dresses so stiff they seemed to be made of metal. She had hard blue eyes like marbles, and smiling was something she almost never did.

' "If you like, I'll cut you out a pattern," my mother went on, "and you can sew your own little animal." She looked through the basket of materials on the sofa beside her. "How about this? We could make a small zebra." She held out a piece of black-and-white striped cotton.

' "Can't I make a velvet rabbit instead?" I asked her.

' "I'm afraid not, Pinny dear. Miss Snow asked for a great many rabbits. It seems they are very popular with the children, and I haven't very much velvet left. I'm sorry."

'I could see it was no use at all. I felt angry and miserable, and determined not to take the least bit of trouble over the zebra. I nearly said I didn't want to make

34

one at all, but I was bored and my mother was busy, so I thought I might just as well sew as do anything else. "I'll try a zebra, then. Will you cut it out for me, please."

'To watch my mother cut something out was a treat. Snip went the silver scissors and there was an ear, snap and there was a leg, snip, snap, snip and there were two identical zebra-shaped pieces lying on the carpet, so life-like that they almost seemed to be prancing away on their tiny hooves. I began to like the zebra a little.

' "Now you must sew all round the edges, dear, neatly, mind you, and leave the tummy open for the stuffing. We'll sew it up at the end."

'I sat on a stool beside my mother and sewed as neatly as I could. I pricked my finger once, in spite of my thimble, and a little drop of blood fell on the material. I rubbed it off at once, but it left a mark. I tried to sew over the stain, but a little bit still showed. I thought: I don't care. It'll be a rotten old zebra, anyway. I stitched and stitched and after a while, my zebra was ready to be stuffed. I showed it to my mother.

' "That's lovely, dear," she said, but she didn't mean it. It was just that she didn't want to hurt my feelings. I thought that maybe it would look better when it had been stuffed, and I said so. My mother looked relieved. "Oh, I'm sure it will. Let's stuff it at once."

'We pushed small pieces of rag into the gaping stomach, and sewed it up. I sewed on two black buttons for eyes, and my mother embroidered a red mouth, and then we looked at it, standing lopsided on the carpet. I burst into tears.

' "Pinny, love, what's the matter? There's your lovely zebra that you made yourself. You should be proud. Why ever are you crying?"

' "When you cut it out it was *really* a zebra, small and prancing and so pretty, but now I've sewn it, it's lumpy and its back is crooked, and its ears aren't the right shape and it can hardly stand, and it's got a spot of my blood on it. I don't like it, and I don't want to keep it."

'In the end, my mother calmed me down with a cup of warm milk, and the promise of a whole sixpence to spend at the jumble sale, on whatever I liked. I went to bed that night and dreamed of my crooked zebra, unable to run through the grass with his real zebra friends.

'Next morning, I gave the zebra to my mother for the Soft Toy Stall, and she was very pleased. "If you don't want it, I'm sure there's some child who will. Thank you, Pinny. I shall tell Miss Snow that it's your contribution, and I shall put it right at the front of the stall."

'I spent the next few days thinking about how I would spend my money. On the day of the jumble sale, my mother wrapped the sixpence in tissue paper, and put it into my pocket. I felt it with my fingers every few minutes as we walked to the Church Hall, just to make certain it was still there, safe.

'The Church Hall looked splendid. Usually, it was a brown and green box with a dusty stage at the far end, full of little draughts of wind that puffed around your feet. But now it was decorated with holly wreaths and red ribbons and paper lanterns, and filled with stalls full of treasures. I didn't know where to look first, and I was standing in the doorway deciding where to go, when Miss Snow in a shiny, steel dress (shiny, because this was an occasion) pushed her way between the stalls towards us. She ignored me completely, but she said to my mother: "Ah, capital, Mrs Pintle. All ready for the fray, I see. Good, good. The public will be arriving in half an hour. Would you be so good as to put the finishing touches to your stall? Thank you so much."

'She gathered her skirts together and ploughed back to where she came from. My mother hurried away. I looked around. Ladies behind each stall were arranging, rearranging, counting out piles of pennies, smoothing their hair, smiling, fluttering fingers to their brooches, waving to one another. One other person was standing about, like me, and that was the Vicar. He was a small, mouse-like man, with soft, white hands and soft, white hair. He came and spoke to me for a while, about how lovely the Hall looked, and how hard everyone had worked, and about what I was going to buy, until Miss Snow towed him away to help sort out the second-hand books. I was left alone to look at everything.

'Some stalls I didn't even stop at. I wasn't interested in pots of home-made jam, or ugly vases, or second-hand baby clothes. I didn't need lace mats, or unpolished brass candlesticks, or pin cushions. My mother's stall was the best. It would have looked like a whole zoo of wonderful animals, if it were not for my zebra right in the front row. I looked at him for a long time. It seemed to me as though the other animals were staring at him out of their button eyes, as if to say: "Whatever are *you* doing here? You should go somewhere else. We are beautiful beasts, while you are not beautiful at all." I was surprised to find myself feeling cross with the other soft toys. I even turned one particularly smug tiger right round, because he was looking so pleased with himself that I didn't want to see his face. I said to the zebra, in a whisper:

"Don't worry, I'm sure someone will want you and buy you very soon."

'As I wandered away, I was quite surprised at what I'd done. Could I be growing fond of the zebra I'd made? It was not really fondness, I decided. I was just feeling a little sorry for it.

'People began to come into the Hall just then, and soon it became filled with voices, and the smell of coats, and the rustle of best dresses. Hats blossomed like flowers against the brown walls, rings

shone in the light, children pulled at skirts, hands touched and picked up, and put down, eyes looked, purses came out of bags, and precious bargains were laid in baskets.

'I stood for a long time near the Dolls' Stall, trying to decide whether I wanted another. Dolls are strange: you either take to them or you don't. These dolls all had pouting mouths, hair that was too yellow, gowns that were too fine. I could not imagine loving a single one of them. I moved on.

'Then I saw it. It was a musical box, playing "Goodbye, Dolly Gray". It was the most enchanting thing I had ever seen, and I wanted it with all my heart. The wooden lid was painted in a pattern of plump, pink flowers and glossy blue ribbons, and right in the middle there was a picture of a lady dancing in a shower of tiny, black notes of music: crotchets, and quavers and semi-quavers. The lady's dress was blue, with a full skirt. As soon as I could make myself heard above the noise, I asked the lady behind the stall how much the musical box cost.

' "What box, dear? Oh, that old thing. That's only a shilling."

'My fingers crushed the sixpence in my pocket. Only half enough. What was I going to do? My mother would have to give me a whole new sixpence. Maybe she wouldn't want to? I pushed that thought away quickly. Surely she would want me to have the lovely box? Would someone else buy it in the time it would take me to walk to the Soft Toy Stall, and back? They were almost bound to, because it was the prettiest thing in the Hall. I decided to stay near the box all afternoon, and touch it whenever anyone came near it. Then they would think I was buying it. As soon as people began to leave the Hall at the end of the afternoon, I would rush back to my mother and ask for the money.

'The time passed quickly. I played

"Goodbye Dolly Gray" over and over again, and hardly noticed the other people. After a while, they began to leave the Hall. Outside it was dark. This, I thought, would be a safe moment to rush to my mother and ask her for another sixpence.

'She was sitting on a chair behind her stall, looking very happy. Her hair was a little untidy, and her cheeks were pink.

' "Mother," I said, "I'm so sorry, but I've found just what I'd like and it costs a shilling. Please, *please* can you give me another sixpence?"

' "Aren't you even going to tell me what it is?" My mother smiled at me.

' "A musical box, with a dancing lady, and flowers. It plays 'Goodbye Dolly Gray'. It's beautiful."

' "Well, it sounds very nice, dear, I'm sure." She pushed some strands of hair away from her forehead. "As I've done so well and sold nearly all my animals, and since it's nearly Christmas, I suppose you

44

may have an extra sixpence, just this once."

'I ran behind the stall, and hugged my mother's knees, while she counted out the money. I looked up. My mother had put six separate pennies out on the red cloth of the stall. I noticed, briefly, that my zebra was the only animal that had not been sold, and I felt a little sad for him, but I was longing to go back to my box, and so happy at the thought of owning it, and stroking it, and hearing the twinkling music in my very own room that I forgot about the zebra as soon as I had collected the six pennies together.

'I fled back to pay for my musical box. It was gone. I looked under the cloth that covered the stall, under embroidered tray cloths, behind all the ornaments lying on the stall. It had gone. I couldn't believe it. I said to the lady: "Please, where is the musical box?"

' "Sold, dear, I'm afraid," she answered, putting things away into brown boxes. "Just a few moments ago. I didn't know you were interested in buying it."

'Again, I could not believe it. Had she not even seen me there, all afternoon, stroking the lid? Had she not heard the music? I stared at the lady's drooping cheeks, and her plum-coloured dress and nearly burst with pure anger. I hated her.

'I walked back to my mother's stall. I didn't know where I was. I forgot about people, and bumped into knees and baskets feeling nothing, feeling numbed. All I knew and all I could think of was the deep, black hole of disappointment and loss that had taken the place of all the pleasure I had felt when I thought I owned the box. Gradually, I began to notice what was around me. I was standing beside my mother's stall, and the zebra was looking up at me, quite kindly, I thought. My misery and the zebra's loneliness on the counter became mixed up together. It seemed that no one else

46

wanted him, so he would be mine, after all. I paid my mother a shilling for him. I didn't need the money for anything now, and I thought it would make the zebra feel more important if he were a bought animal, and not simply a leftover. I pulled him off the stall and hugged him. He was soft and comforting. Then I went and sat on the steps by the side of the stage, out of sight of my mother, and wept and wept into the zebra's black-and-white back.

'I don't know how long I sat there, crying, but after a while, I noticed a shiny pair of black boots on the floor, buttoned firmly around two short legs. Then came a cherry-red skirt, trimmed with white fur, a tight red jacket, with fur at the neck and wrists, and then a face. The face belonged to a girl, with round cheeks and a straight fringe of dark hair. Her eyes were brown and bright and very wide open. She was chewing her bottom lip, and clutching a white fur muff. The string dangled and dragged on the dirty floor.

47

She said: "You've been crying for ages."

' "Yes," I managed to mutter.

' "Have you finished crying now?"

' "I think so, thank you. I'll cry again later."

' "Why are you crying, anyway? I wouldn't cry, not with a zebra like that."

' "Do you like it?"

' "Yes," said the girl firmly. "I like animals. I like sick animals best, because then I can play animal hospitals, which is my favourite game. Your zebra looks *very* sick. That's why I like him."

' "I made him," I said.

' "Oh, my!" (the brown eyes opened wider) "how clever of you, to make a sick zebra."

' "You can have him. I don't really want him. I only took him because I felt sorry for him. Nobody bought him, you see."

' "I would've, if I'd seen him," said the girl. "Thank you, though, very much, for giving him to me. My name is Helen Arthur. What's your name?"

' "Pinny," I said. "Well, Penelope Sophia Pintle, really, but that's long, so I'm called Pinny."

' "I haven't very much I can give you in return, I'm afraid. Only a silly little box thing my Nanny bought for me." From her muff she took out my box, with the dancing lady on it, and almost threw it into my lap.

'I think Helen was very surprised when I jumped up and hugged her. I was quite surprised myself. I almost shouted: "Oh, I love you, Helen, I love you. You're my friend! You are my friend, aren't you?"

' "I don't really know you, but you look nice. I will be your friend if you like."

' "We held hands and went over to where my mother was putting her coat on.

' "Is that your mother?" asked Helen.

' "Yes, in the brown dress."

49

' "She's talking to my Nanny."

' "Haven't you got a mother?" I wanted to know.

' "Yes, but she goes out a lot, so Nanny looks after me most of the time."

'I went up to my mother, and told her about Helen giving me the musical box. Helen said to her Nanny: "Please can Pinny come to tea tomorrow?" And, of course, Nanny said "yes" and my mother said "yes".'

Aunt Pinny got up.

'Is that the end of the story,' I murmured.

'Yes, and the beginning of my friendship with Helen. We've been friends ever since. She's an elderly lady now, like me, I suppose. But she looks just the same to me as she did then, so many years ago. She still wears a cherry-red coat.'

'But how did you come to have the patch for your quilt, if Helen had the zebra?'

Aunt Pinny laughed. 'Zebra was operated on in Helen's animal hospital almost immediately. We cut a big piece out of his side and replaced it with a bit of red felt. That was the scar, you see. I kept the cut-out black-and-white piece and sewed it into the quilt. Goodnight, now.'

Aunt Pinny switched off the light and went out of the room.

This story is by Adèle Geras.

Greedy Gregory's Tooth

Greedy Gregory's tooth had been loose for days. At school while he was meant to be learning his tables, Greedy Gregory pushed at the tooth with his tongue. When he ate his lunch he would bite down hard on his choo-choo bar, hoping that the tooth would come out. It did get stuck in a lump of Jersey toffee once, but Greedy Gregory was too scared to tug it out – he had to wait half an hour for the toffee to dissolve.

Walking home from school, he twisted the tooth back and forth with his dirty fingers but, even though it was only hanging by a thread, it still wouldn't come out.

Then, late one afternoon, his sister caught him by surprise with a kung-fu kick to the jaw. He was just about to counter-attack when he felt the tooth – it was lying on his tongue, just behind his bottom teeth, and there was a big spongy lump where his tooth used to be.

'Maaam, Daaad!' he yelled.

'You sook!' said his little sister. 'I hardly touched you . . .'

But Greedy Gregory pushed past her and ran into the kitchen.

'Mum! Dad! Look at me toof. What a beauty!'

Greedy Gregory's dad took down a glass and filled it up with water. 'Put your tooth in that,' he said, 'and we'll see what the tooth fairy brings you tonight.'

Greedy Gregory dropped the tooth into the glass of water and held it up to the light. The tooth looked even bigger through the glass.

'A toof like that must be worth at least a dollar,' said Greedy Gregory.

'Don't be funny,' said his dad. 'You'll be lucky to get five cents for it – it's got a great big hole in it. Not to mention the colour.'

Greedy Gregory scowled at his dad. 'That toof fairy had better give me a dollar or I'll smash 'er,' he said, and he went off to the bathroom to count the rest of his teeth. His sister followed him and watched while he stood in front of the mirror and opened his mouth wide. It was not a pretty sight. All his teeth were green or grey, and bits of his lunch were still stuck in the gaps.

'Un, ooo, eee, or, ive, ix . . .' Greedy Gregory counted all his teeth, top and bottom – incisors, canine teeth and molars – then he multiplied by a dollar (the one-times table was the only one he could remember).

'I'll be rich!' he cried. 'Twenty dollars! Think of all the lollies I can buy with twenty dollars!' And he counted his teeth all over again, just to be sure.

'You won't get a dollar a tooth for those horrible green things,' said his sister, and marched off to practise her karate.

'Just you wait and see,' he yelled. 'If I don't get a dollar a toof, that fairy'd better watch out,' and he pulled his most ferocious face.

That night, Greedy Gregory went to bed extra early to wait for the tooth fairy. He put the glass of water on his bedside table and stared at the tooth. It did look a bit green in the lamplight. There was a dark brown hole in one side, but Greedy Gregory was sure it was worth more than five cents. It was such a *big* tooth, and besides, it was *his*. I'll stay awake till the toof fairy comes, he thought, and if she tries to leave me anything less than a dollar I'll . . . *yawn*. Greedy Gregory's eyes began to close, and his head sank on to his chest.

55

'*Ping!*' Something long and hard and springy landed on Gregory's head.

'Uh – what . . .?' Greedy Gregory blinked. There was a funny blue light in the room. He rubbed his eyes.

'I said *ping!*'

Gregory looked up, and up, and up. The biggest tooth fairy he had ever seen was standing beside his bed, whacking him on the head with her wand.

'Are you Greedy Gregory?' she snapped.

'Yes I am.'

'And this is your tooth?'

'Yes it is,' said Greedy Gregory.

'Right,' said the fairy, tucking her wand under her arm and plonking herself down on the bed. 'How much do you want for it?'

Gregory wished she'd move over a bit – she was squashing his legs. His knees felt as if they might bend back the wrong way at any moment.

'Come on – don't muck about,' said the

56

fairy. 'Do you know how many kids I have to see tonight?'

'I want a dollar,' said Greedy Gregory.

'Nothing doing,' said the fairy. 'The going rate is five cents.'

'Not for Gregory Grabham's teef,' he replied firmly.

'Oh, indeed? Pardon me,' said the fairy. 'I thought we were talking about this nasty green object.' The fairy prodded the tooth with her wand. 'Gregory Grabham's *teeth*,' she added, 'are a different matter.' And she began to do some quick calculations.

Greedy Gregory leant back on his pillow and watched the fairy filling in some figures in a little book. Fairies are all the same, he thought smugly, treat them tough and they give you what you want.

'This is the first tooth you've ever lost?' asked the fairy.

'Yes.'

'So, counting this tooth, you've got twenty teeth altogether?'

'That's right,' said Gregory. The fairy was obviously no fool – she knew how much she'd have to pay for a Gregory Grabham tooth. He began to imagine the sweets and ice creams he'd be able to buy tomorrow.

'Right,' said the fairy, under her breath. 'Twenty teeth at five cents a tooth makes a dollar.' (The fairy knew her five-times table back to front.)

Greedy Gregory was so busy thinking of food that he only heard the last bit: '. . . a tooth makes a dollar'.

'That's right,' he said firmly. 'I'll take nothing less than a dollar.'

'All right,' said the fairy, 'a dollar it is. Sign here.' And she held out the book for Gregory to sign with a special magic pencil that wrote everything in triplicate.

Greedy Gregory was so eager to get his dollar that he signed straight away without reading a word of the contract.

'Done!' said the fairy, shutting the book with a bang. 'Now, open your mouth.'

'What?' cried Gregory.

'Open your mouth!' said the fairy. 'Don't muck about.'

'Why should I?' said Greedy Gregory.

The fairy was getting impatient, and her face was getting redder and redder. 'Look,' she said, 'we made a deal. You get your dollar and I get your teeth.'

'My *what*?' squeaked Gregory.

'Your teeth, dumbskull. Now open your mouth.'

Greedy Gregory went very pale. 'But . . . but . . .' he stammered, 'I thought it was a dollar a toof.'

'Don't be wet,' said the fairy. 'A dollar for *that*! Look at it.' She picked the tooth up gingerly between her finger and thumb, and held it under Gregory's nose. 'It's *green*! she snapped. 'It hasn't been cleaned for *months*! And it's got a big ugly *hole* in one side. What use is a tooth like that?'

Greedy Gregory stared at his tooth. It didn't look too good, jammed between the fairy's big freckly fingers. A drop of dirty water fell off the end of the tooth and soaked into the sheet. Gregory began to cry.

'Now look here,' said the fairy, 'no crying – it was all fair and square. You want a dollar, right? At five cents a tooth, multiplied by twenty teeth, you get a dollar. Now I can't say fairer than that.'

Gregory wished he'd practised his five-times tables. His teacher was right – you never knew when you might need them.

The fairy reached into a bag she had slung over her back and pulled out an enormous pair of pliers. 'Come on now,' she said gruffly, 'I can't muck around all night.'

Greedy Gregory felt sick. 'I don't want a dollar,' he snivelled, staring at the huge pliers. 'I want to keep my teef!'

The fairy waved the pliers at Gregory. 'Look, kid – we made a deal and you signed it fair and square.'

'But I want to un-make it,' sobbed
Gregory.

'Can't un-make a deal,' said the fairy
sternly. 'All you can do is make a new
one.'

'Yes! Yes!' he cried. 'Anything.'

The fairy pulled out another book and
flipped through the pages. 'Well,' she

said, 'You haven't got much to offer me – unless your teeth improve a bit. Perhaps Form CT.20 might do the trick.'

Greedy Gregory wiped his eyes and peered at the form. This time he read every word – even the fine print at the bottom of the page. Here is what it said:

'I,......................., do solemnly swear to take good care of all my teeth, to visit the dentist every six months, and to brush my teeth after every meal. Signed..........................

And in the small print at the bottom:

'I also promise not to eat too many lollies or ice creams or sweet biscuits.'

Gregory signed.

Next morning, Gregory woke late. His eyes were all puffy and he felt awful. He ran his tongue over his teeth. Thank goodness – they were all there, just as furry and dirty as they were last night. He raced into the bathroom and grabbed a toothbrush.

'Did you look in your tooth glass?' asked his mum as he scrubbed away at his teeth. 'The tooth fairy left you something.'

Gregory walked slowly back into his room. There on the sheet was the dirty mark where the tooth fairy had dropped a little water the night before. Greedy Gregory hardly dared to look in the glass. What if there were a dollar coin at the bottom – would she come back another night with her pliers and pull out all his teeth?

But there at the bottom of the glass was a shiny silver five-cent coin.

'Look, Mum,' said Gregory, 'five cents!' And he gave his mother a big, white, gleaming smile.

This story is by Nan McNab.

Croup, the Sea-dog

On a big black rock in the middle of the sea stood a red-and-white striped lighthouse. This was the home of the little lighthouse keeper, Ray.

At first, Ray had wanted to be a sailor, but whenever he went to sea, he was seasick. So then he got the job of lighthouse keeper on the big black rock, and he had been there ever since.

He was never lonely. Seabirds came to rest on the rock. Seals clambered up on to it to sunbathe. Puffins and gannets dived off it for fish. And, of course, there was his dog, Croup.

Croup was fat and furry, and followed Ray everywhere. Ray first called him Croup after hearing him bark. (If you say 'croup' out loud, rather gruffly, you'll know exactly how he sounded — just like someone with a bad cough.)

'Come on, Croup,' said Ray every morning. 'Time to see to the Light.'

One morning, Ray set off up the ninety-six spiral stairs which led to the very top of the lighthouse. Croup followed him with a little jerky jump up each stair. They were both puffing a little when they reached the top. Here was the Light Room, where the huge Light shone all night long. It warned ships to keep well away from the big black rock that stuck up sharply out of the sea. Ray inspected the Light.

'Seems all ship-shape.' He nodded.

Then he polished the windows which went all round the Light Room.

'Bit of a mist over the water today,' he

65

said to Croup. 'Hope we're not going to have one of those foggy spells. Ah, well, if we do, I'll have to switch on the fog horn. We don't want any ships crashing on to the black rock in the dark.'

Ray went down the spiral stairs, and Croup lolloped after him, a step at a time. They reached the ground and walked outside. Ray looked out across the water.

'It's very still today,' he said. 'I don't like it. I can't even hear the seabirds. And the mist is getting thicker.'

'Croup, croup,' barked Croup, and the echo went all round the lighthouse.

Ray shivered. 'I don't like mist at all,' he said. 'And sailors don't like it either. They hate sailing in fog when they can't see a thing.'

By evening the fog was really thick. Ray and Croup stood at the door of the lighthouse. Everything was very still. They could hear the faint swish of the sea, but they couldn't see it. There was nothing but whiteness all around.

Ray switched on the Light and the fog horn. A great beam of light shone into the whiteness. The fog horn started to sound. (If you sing 'Durr . . . durr' aloud, then count to six in your head and sing 'Durr . . . durr' again, you'll know exactly what it sounded like.)

Ray and Croup ate their supper.

'I hope those ships out there can hear our fog horn,' said Ray.

Croup didn't answer. He was eating his favourite meaty snacks.

Suddenly Ray said, 'Hey! Did you hear that?'

Croup looked up.

'The fog horn's stopped,' cried Ray. 'I'll have to try and mend it. But how can we warn ships off the rock? They'll never see the light in this fog.'

'Croup, croup,' barked Croup anxiously.

'Yes, yes,' said Ray, 'you've got a lovely loud bark, old fellow. They'd be able to hear you all right. They'd hear you miles away.'

'Croup, croup!' barked Croup again, as loudly as he could.

Ray looked at his furry fat friend again – and suddenly realized what he was saying. 'Ah, yes, old fellow, you *have* got a good strong bark. They certainly *would* hear you miles away. Do you think you could keep barking while I mend the fog horn?'

Croup answered with a wag of his tail
and made for the door. Ray opened it for
him. Croup went out into the fog and sat
at the edge of the rock.

Ray wrapped a thick rug round him.
'Stay there then, old fellow,' he said. 'I'm
off to mend the fog horn.'

'Croup . . . croup,' barked Croup into
the whiteness. He counted up to six in his
head, then barked again, 'Croup . . .
croup.' It sounded just like someone with
a bad cough, and it echoed out into the
thick fog.

Not very far off, a ship was sailing
very slowly through the fog. There was

whiteness all around. The captain looked at his chart.

'Somewhere near here,' he said, 'there's a big rock with a lighthouse on it. I hope we don't crash into it. We can't see a thing in this fog.'

'Can't hear anything either,' said the mate.

They both strained their ears.

Suddenly the captain heard a faint sound, then another. 'Did you cough?' he asked the mate.

'Cough, sir? No, sir,' said the mate, looking puzzled.

They strained their ears again. There was another faint sound, followed by another.

'Did you cough, sir?' asked the mate.

'Me, mate?' said the captain. 'No, mate.'

They both listened again.

'It's someone coughing,' said the mate.

'Must be on the big rock,' said the captain. 'We must be very near it.'

'We'd better stop sailing then,' said the mate.

'We'll drop anchor here,' said the captain. 'We can stay here safely until morning light.'

The mate nodded. 'Perhaps the fog will have cleared by then.'

'There it goes again,' said the captain. 'It's a terrible cough.'

'Good thing we heard it in time,' said the mate.

They lowered the anchor and went to sleep in their bunks.

When the sun came up the next morning, the fog had cleared. The sky was blue and gold, and the sea was silver.

'There's the lighthouse rock, just over there,' shouted the captain, coming up on deck. 'Good thing we didn't sail any nearer.'

'We might have had a dreadful crash,' agreed the mate.

'I can still hear that coughing sound,' said the captain.

'But it's very faint now,' the mate replied.

'It's coming from the rock,' said the captain. 'From that red thing on the rock.' He looked through the binoculars. 'Well, bless my barnacles,' he cried. 'It's a dog wrapped in a red rug! Here, take a look, mate!'

At that moment the real fog horn boomed out across the sea: 'Durr . . . durr.' Ray had mended it at last. He raced down the spiral stairs and out on to the rock.

There sat fat little Croup, just where he had left him. He was very cold, and his voice had nearly gone. Ray picked him up and carried him back inside. Soon Ray had a roaring fire going, and Croup was sitting in front of it, crunching a bowl of meaty snacks.

'Yum, yum,' he thought. 'This is better than sitting on a flat rock with a cold bot all night.'

'I'll put a drop of rum in your water

72

bowl,' said Ray. 'You're a real sea-dog, old fellow, a real sea-dog.'

'Croup,' whispered Croup happily, and thumped his tail on the floor.

This story is by Margaret Joy.

Cherry Pie

An old man and his wife lived together in a hut among the mountains. They were poor and hard-working, but contented, and when they sat by the fire at night, the old man smoking his pipe and the old woman knitting, there was nothing in the wide world they wished for — except just one thing which they had given up hope of having, and that was a child of their own.

All the children who lived in the mountain village loved the old couple and on their way to school they would tap on the window of the hut and wave as they went by. On their way home, the old woman would sometimes beckon them in and give them a new, crisp biscuit, shaped like a shamrock leaf, or half a rosy apple. The old man was never too busy to mend the strap of a pair of skates or sew a buckle on a leather school bag.

At Christmas time, the old man and woman liked to give a present to every child in the village, from the babies to the big boys ready to go out into the world. They were so poor that they had to make the presents themselves. They made them of wool which they got from a relation who kept sheep down in the valley. The old woman spun the wool and the old man dyed it bright colours.

Together they made woolly balls for the babies, mufflers and caps for the big children, and dolls for the ones in be-tween. Even the little boys were pleased with a doll dressed like a shepherd or a sailor.

One Christmas, when the presents

75

were all finished, the old woman set to work on something else. It was a big doll, as big as a real child.

'What are you doing?' asked the old man.

'I am making us a little boy,' she replied.

His hair was made of dozens of loops of yellow wool and he had blue eyes and red cheeks. She dressed him in a red jersey and navy trousers and soft felt slippers. The old man made him a leather belt and a little wooden stool to sit on. As he sat on his stool by the fire, his legs looked exactly as if he were alive, warming his feet in their neat grey slippers.

'If only he were really alive!' sighed the old woman. 'If only he could speak and eat and play about! How happy I should be!'

On Christmas Eve they decided to take their child to the Wishing Well at midnight. The well was named the Well of Saint Nicholas and it was believed that anyone visiting it at midnight on Christmas Eve would have a wish granted. They wrapped the doll in a blanket and carried him to the well. It was a long, cold trudge, the snow sparkling with frost and the stars so large and bright that they seemed no higher than the church spire.

The well was frozen over and the old man broke the ice with a stone before they could dip their fingers in the freezing water and make the sign of the cross.

'Blessed Saint Nicholas, who loves the little ones, grant life to the child we have made.'

As they hurried home, their faces numb with cold, the old man thought he felt something stirring inside the blanket. When they were back in the hut, with the door shut, he set the doll down and at once he began capering round the room, dancing and jumping, stopping every now and then to hug and kiss his new father and mother.

The old people's joy was beyond

words. They laughed and cried and kissed each other while the old woman prepared a bed beside their own. It was nearly morning before the child seemed tired and allowed himself to be put to bed by his new mother. He fell asleep at once, though his parents hardly closed their eyes as they got up so often to make sure he was still there, breathing gently, his yellow head half buried in the pillow.

Now life in the hut was very different. The child was always playing about and getting into mischief. He tangled his mother's knitting and hid his father's tobacco and spilt food on his red jersey. But his parents loved him far too much to be angry.

At first he could not speak, though he soon learned to understand what was said to him; then one day, at dinner, he said plainly, 'Cherry pie,' which was what he was eating. These were his first words and his parents called him Cherry Pie from that moment.

Cherry Pie loved the other children who came to marvel at him and he soon showed, by signs, that he wanted strong boots and a leather jacket such as they wore, so he could romp outside in the snow. His mother tried to keep him indoors where he was safe, but he pined and refused to eat and spent all day gazing out of the window. His rosy cheeks faded, and fearing that he would become ill, his parents gave him the boots and jacket he wanted, and a cap and gloves too, and he ran out into the snow to play with his friends.

Sliding, sledging, skiing, skating, Cherry Pie could do them all as well, or better, than the others and he soon learned to talk as fast as the others too. He begged to go to school and when he heard the school bell ringing he cried and sobbed till his father made him a school satchel and he went off every morning with his dinner inside, wrapped in a clean cloth.

Now Cherry Pie was a real boy. He

could talk as well as everyone else and join in their games and learn his lessons.

'He's a real boy!' sighed his mother happily, as she darned a tear in his jersey.

'He's a real boy, a tough little fellow!' added his father proudly. 'He can hold his own even with the bigger ones.'

'He's just like us,' said the other children when they went home after school. 'He's just the same except that he doesn't feel hot or cold as we do, and if he pricks himself, sawdust comes out instead of blood.'

But they were all wrong, the father and mother and the children. Cherry Pie was not just like the others. He was different. At first only the priest knew. His mother went to the priest to ask him to christen Cherry Pie and she was bitterly disappointed when he refused.

'Bring him to church — let him read the Bible — let him sing hymns with his friends — but I do not feel I can christen him. I cannot be sure that he knows the difference between right and wrong.'

'Indeed he does, Father,' said Cherry Pie's mother. 'If he has been up to mischief he hides when I come in. He knows he has been disobedient.'

'Maybe! Maybe! But I'd like to wait before I receive him into the Holy Church. You're a good woman and you mustn't fret. Go on loving him and bringing him up carefully.'

Sometimes the children at school and,

indeed, everyone who knew Cherry Pie, were surprised at him. He would kick a kitten out of the way with his foot and when the other children said: 'Don't do that. You'll hurt it!' Cherry Pie said 'All right,' and he never did it again. Another day he would knock a smaller child over in a game and go on playing as if nothing had happened. When the others called out: 'Look what you've done! Her knee is bleeding!' he would pick the child up and never be rough with her again. But that same day he might throw a boy's book into the stove and when his friends cried out: 'How can he do his homework? What will he do without his book?' Cherry Pie would give the boy his own book, and would never again repeat that cruel trick.

Once he laughed to see a dead bird in the snow and Franz, his best friend, said to him: 'Have a heart, Cherry Pie. Aren't you sad to see it cold and stiff?'

Cherry Pie ran home and asked his

mother eagerly: 'Have I a heart, mother?'

'No dear, you haven't,' she replied.

'Why not? Why haven't I a heart like everyone else? Tell me why!'

'I suppose I forgot to make one for you.'

'Then make one now, this minute?' For the first time Cherry Pie was in a rage and stamped his feet and shouted 'Make one now, before you cook the supper. I must have a heart.'

His mother quietly looked out her work basket and some red flannel and made him a heart. He stood in silence, watching every stitch.

'Put it inside me, in the proper place,' he ordered, when the heart was finished.

'But it might hurt you. I — I don't think I can do it. Please don't make me, Cherry Pie.'

'You must do it,' said Cherry Pie sternly. 'You must. If you don't I shall run away and never come back. I can't live here without a heart.'

So his mother took out her scissors and her needle and thread and her thimble, and she put the heart inside him in its proper place, and sewed him up again. He never moved or spoke till she had finished. Then he jumped for joy and threw his arms round her neck.

'Mother,' he said as he hugged her, 'what is it I feel beating against me when you hold me close?'

'It is my heart beating.'

Cherry Pie put his hand over his own chest and a puzzled look came over his face.

'My heart is still and quiet. It doesn't beat. Why doesn't it beat like yours?'

'I don't know, my little pigeon,' said his mother tenderly. 'I cannot tell. I would do anything in the world to please you and so would your father, but we cannot make your heart beat.'

Cherry Pie grew bigger like the other village children and did more difficult lessons at school and was more useful at home, helping to chop the wood and sweep the snow from the doorstep. Now and then he still hurt someone's feelings without knowing it, though he was sorry when it was explained to him. 'I didn't know,' he would say. 'I never thought — It never occurred to me.'

Kittens and puppies and very small children kept out of his way and hid when they saw him coming. He never knew why. He did not wish to harm them. Yet somehow he frightened them and upset them. He knew that he had a heart because he had seen his mother making it, but it did not seem to tell him what to do as it should.

One summer's day, Cherry Pie was walking by himself on the mountainside when he heard a sad bleating. Looking round, he saw a young kid that had somehow become separated from its mother. The little thing ran to him hopefully and began to suck his fingers and the sleeve of his jersey.

'Poor little thing, you're lost and hungry,' said Cherry Pie. 'I'll take you back to the herd and we'll soon find your mother. She'll feed you and comfort you.'

He tried to coax the kid to follow him but the track was rough and stony and he found he had to carry it. Small though it was, it was heavier than he thought possible and he had to stop and rest many times before he reached the grassy alp where the goats were feeding. The kid ran bleating to its mother who was calling loudly for her lost child.

As Cherry Pie went back to the hut for his dinner, he felt a strange, warm glow. He even pushed up his sleeves and loosened the button at his collar. It was a new feeling, new and pleasant.

Another day, Cherry Pie was crouching behind a boulder, watching a chamois and her young one leaping from rock to rock. The mother went first and if the leap was very wide she waited for the young one, turning her head to encourage

86

it and licking it when it was once again beside her. They were so beautiful that Cherry Pie could have watched all day. Their slender legs looked too fragile to bear them as they leapt and frolicked as if they had wings.

Suddenly he noticed that he was not alone. Two hunters were watching also. They held guns in their hands and had hunting knives hung at their belts. He could see the green tassels on their hats and the intent look on their faces.

Cherry Pie only knew the chamois were in danger and he ran forward, waving his arms and shouting. In a second the two animals were out of sight. He did not wait to hear the angry words of the huntsmen. He hurried home feeling, for the second time, a lovely glow of warmth.

'How rosy your cheeks are!' said his mother when he got back to the hut.

Some days later Cherry Pie was out for a walk with his friend Franz. Cherry Pie was wearing a pair of new boots his father had made. They had clusters of nails on the soles so he would not slip and the laces were tough leather thongs. The nails made patterns where the snow was soft. He felt proud as he strode along, proud of his stout, strong boots such as big boys wore.

The two boys climbed higher and higher above the village and nearer to the great glacier, the Sea of Glass, which was famous for many miles around.

'Shall we turn back?' said Franz. 'I've never been as high as this without my father.'

'Nor have I,' said Cherry Pie, 'but let's go on a little way. Let's go to the edge of the Sea of Glass and just set foot on it. Then we'll turn back.'

'We haven't a rope,' said Franz, 'or an ice axe. Perhaps we should turn back now.'

'Oh, we're all right,' said Cherry Pie.

'My new boots won't slip. They can't slip, they're so well nailed.'

'My boots aren't new,' muttered Franz. 'They're old and the nails are worn down.'

'I'll hold your hand and then you'll feel safe,' said Cherry Pie.

The Sea of Glass was so beautiful that the boys were glad they had come so far. It was blue and shone so brightly that they had to screw up their eyes. They tried a few steps on its polished surface, Cherry Pie going first, but almost at once Franz gave a cry of terror and there was a crackling, slithering sound. He had fallen down a crevasse, a deep crack in the ice.

Cherry Pie lay flat and peered over the edge. It was dark and horrible, but he could see Franz's blue cap far below.

'Are you all right, Franz?'

'Yes. I'm caught on a ledge but it's very narrow.'

'Hold on. I'll let down my scarf and pull you up.'

Cherry Pie unwound the long warm scarf his mother had knitted and lowered it down the crack.

'Can you reach the end, Franz?'

'No,' came Franz's voice. 'No. It isn't long enough.'

Cherry Pie undid the leather belt his father had made and fixed it on to the scarf. He lowered this down the crevasse.

'Hold on, Franz.'

The answer came more faintly. 'I can't quite reach.'

Cherry Pie thought quickly. What could he add to his home-made rope? A sock, perhaps? His jersey? Then he remembered his leather boot-laces. Fumbling in his hurry he undid one lace, then the other, and knotted them on to the end. This time Franz's voice said, 'Yes. I've got it. I'm holding on.'

'I'm going to pull you up,' said Cherry Pie, but he found that he was not strong

90

enough. He could not raise Franz an inch.

'You must hold on to your end and I'll hold on to mine,' said Cherry Pie. 'Someone will pass by and they will help. Just hold on.'

Both boys held on, knowing that few people passed that way, especially in winter. It was a lucky chance that the priest went by, as dusk was gathering, having visited a sick woman in the next village.

He was able to rescue Franz and carry him home, Cherry Pie stumbling along beside him. Stiff and numb though he was, he felt the strange warmth spreading even to his icy hands and feet.

When he lay in front of the fire, wrapped in blankets, his father and mother rubbing him and petting him, he suddenly cried out: 'My heart is beating! My heart is beating at last! Father! Mother! Feel it beating! That's why I felt warm even when I was lying on the ice.'

Now the family in the hut had nothing else to wish for. They did not need to visit St Nicholas's Well again. The priest gladly christened Cherry Pie and from that time he never hurt anyone's feelings and the little children and animals ran to meet him, instead of hiding. His red flannel heart worked as well as everyone else's and told him what to do.

This story is by Ruth Ainsworth.

Simple Jack

Jack lived with his mother in a cottage beside a common. He was the laziest boy in the world. His mother earned a living for them both by spinning, and when she wasn't spinning she was washing or mending, and when she wasn't washing or mending she was getting a meal ready. But all Jack would do was to sit under the apple tree in summer sucking grasses, and in the chimney corner in winter keeping his toes warm.

At last his mother could put up with it no longer.

'Out you go,' said she one fine Monday morning. 'Out you go, and earn yourself a living or you shan't stay here any more. You're old enough to get work for yourself now, so don't come back till you've made some money to help pay for the food you eat!'

Slowly Jack got up from his seat by the fire and went out. He hired himself to a farmer, and by the end of the day he had earned sixpence. Holding it in his hand, he started for home; but, crossing over a brook, he slipped on a wet stone and dropped the sixpence. It was nowhere to be found. There was nothing for it but to go home and tell his mother what had happened.

'Why, you stupid boy!' said his mother. 'I could have done with sixpence, but now you've lost it. You should have put it in your pocket. Then you'd have kept it safe and sound. See if you can do better tomorrow.'

Well, on Tuesday morning Jack went off once more, though he would rather have sat by the fire all day. This time he hired himself to a dairyman, and at the end of the day he was given a pail of milk for wages. So, remembering what his mother had said, he emptied the pail into the pocket of his coat and began to jog along home. Of course the milk was all wasted, and his clothes were soaked into the bargain.

'Why, you silly, good-for-nothing scamp!' cried his mother, when he told her what had happened. 'We could have done with some nice new milk for supper, but now there's none — thanks to your foolishness. You should have carried the pail on your head, then you would have brought it home safe and sound.'

On Wednesday morning Jack went off again to work for the farmer, and for his day's work the farmer gave him a fine pat of butter.

'Now, what did she tell me to do with it?' thought Jack. Then he remembered. He clapped the butter on top of his head and started for home. But it was a warm evening, and soon the butter got stuck in his hair and ran down behind his ears, and some of it fell to the ground, and all of it was spoilt.

Jack's mother was angrier than ever.

'It's too bad!' she said. 'I could have done with some good dairy butter if you hadn't gone and spoilt it all. What a donkey you are! Whatever did you put it on your head for? You should have carried it in your hand.'

Well, on Thursday morning Jack set off once more, trudging away across the common to see a baker in the village; and all day he worked for the baker, and the baker gave him nothing but a black cat for his day's work. He had too many cats in the bakery and was glad to get rid of one.

When he got home, he had nothing at all to show for his day's work except a pair of hands covered all over with bites and scratches.

'What did you get today?' asked Jack's mother.

'Why, the baker gave me a black cat, mother,' said Jack, 'and I carried her in my hands like you told me yesterday, and she scratched me till I had to let her go.'

'Deary me, deary me!' said his mother. 'Aren't you the stupidest ninny ever born? You shouldn't have tried to carry a cat home in your hands. You should have tied a string round her neck and pulled her along after you. It's very vexing,' she went on. 'We could have done with a good cat to keep the mice from the larder!'

On Friday morning Jack went off to the butcher's shop and hired himself to the butcher for the day. Now the butcher was a kind man and knew that Jack's mother was poor, so at the end of the day he gave Jack a leg of good lean mutton. Jack thanked the butcher and left the shop. He thought very carefully about what his mother had told him the day before, and this time he was determined to make no mistake. So he took a piece of string from

his pocket and pulled the meat along behind him in the road.

When she saw the meat, all dirty and spoilt, Jack's mother was more annoyed than ever.

'Oh, you dunderhead!' she cried. 'When *will* you learn sense? We could have done with a fine lean leg of mutton for dinner tomorrow and you've as good as thrown it away! Fancy bringing it home like that!'

'But what *should* I have done, mother?' Jack asked.

'If you'd had two penn'orth of common sense, you'd have lifted it on your shoulder and carried it home like that. Be off to bed with you, for there's not a bite of supper in the house. The way you're going on, we shall both starve, and that's the truth!'

Well, next morning was Saturday, and once more Jack set out to see what he could earn. He hired himself to a cowman that he knew, and at the end of the day the cowman gave him a donkey. So remembering once more what his mother had told him, Jack hoisted the donkey on to his shoulders, and staggered off home. The animal gave poor Jack a great deal of trouble, for it did not like being carried upside down on his shoulders. However, Jack was determined to get home safely *this* time, and not lose his day's wages. So he grasped the donkey's legs with all his strength and took no notice of its braying and kicking.

Now it so happened that in a great house beside the high road lived a rich man, and he had one beautiful daughter who was both deaf and dumb. She had never heard or spoken a word in all her life. But the doctor had told her father that, if the girl could be made to laugh, she might be cured. And the rich man had spent years and years trying to make his beautiful daughter laugh, but the harder he tried the sadder she looked, till everyone gave up hope of ever having her cured.

As Jack was passing the house with the donkey upside down on his back, it happened that the girl was looking out of an upstairs window. Never had she seen such a thing in all her life! There must surely be nothing funnier in the world than to see a great country lad staggering along the road with a donkey kicking and braying upside down on his back: at first the girl could not believe her eyes, and then she began to smile, and then her smile grew broader and broader until she laughed out loud; she laughed so loud and long that the tears came to her eyes, and scarcely knowing what she was doing, she called out to everyone in the house:

'Oh, c–come and look! J–just come and look! Did you ever see such a thing? It's the funniest thing you ever saw!'

Well, the girl's father and all their friends were delighted that at last the girl had spoken, and they were so pleased that they ran out into the road and called Jack inside. So in he went, donkey and all, and the girl was so pleased with him that she wouldn't let him go.

Nothing would please the rich man's daughter but that she should marry Jack and have him to live with for always. And very happy they were in a great house which the rich man bought for them. They kept the donkey in a field at the back of the house, and Jack's mother came to live with them for the rest of her life. Jack became a fine gentleman and had servants to wait on him and see that he never did any more work from that time on.

This story is by James Reeves.

King Midas and His Gold

Once upon a time there was a king called Midas. He was very rich. He lived in a marble palace decorated with gold. He had a golden throne to sit on and a golden crown to wear on his head.

He had chests full of treasures — golden necklaces, golden bracelets, and golden rings. Inside his palace he had trees made by clever craftsmen, with gold and silver leaves. The fruit that hung from the branches was made of precious jewels. Emerald and ruby, amethyst and topaz and lapis lazuli.

One day, the men who worked in

Midas's garden found an old, shabby man asleep among the rose bushes. They tied his hands and feet with garlands of roses, and carried him as their prisoner to King Midas.

'Who are you? And what are you doing in my garden?' Midas asked the man.

'Great King, the god of wine, Dionysus, has many followers. I am one of them. I am old Silenus. If you will set me free so that I can join him again, I will tell you the most wonderful stories you have ever heard.'

Midas kept Silenus in his palace for five days and nights, and he listened to his stories.

'I will tell you,' said Silenus, 'how there is a great land, far away beyond the sea. It is full of splendid cities, and the people who live there are happy and tall and they live nearly for ever. Or shall I tell you about the terrible whirlpool which no human has ever been able to cross?

'Nearby are two streams, and on the

banks of the streams grow two different kinds of tree. The man who eats the fruit of the first kind becomes miserable and he cries and groans until he dies. The man who eats the fruit of the second kind of tree grows younger every day. Even old men can become babies again.'

After hearing these stories, Midas let Silenus go.

The god Dionysus sent a message to Midas. 'I will reward you for looking after my old friend. Tell me what your dearest wish is and I will grant it.'

Midas said at once, 'I should like best that everything I touch should turn into gold.'

'Think carefully what you are asking for,' Dionysus said.

But Midas would not stop to think. He wanted to be the richest man in the world.

Dionysus said, 'Then I will grant your wish. From now on, you have the Golden Touch.'

Midas was delighted. He touched the

stone bench in the garden. It immediately turned into gold. He picked up a pebble from the ground, and found that he held a nugget of gold.

'Wonderful! I shall have a golden palace! I will have a forest of golden trees! Everything around me will be made of gold!' Midas said.

He went round his palace and his garden, turning stone and wood and marble into gold. The roses now had heavy golden blossoms and leaves, on golden stems stiff with golden thorns.

Presently Midas was hungry and thirsty. He went into his palace and sat at his table. He called to his servants to bring him a cup of wine. He was delighted when he saw that as his fingers touched the cup, it turned into a golden goblet.

But as his tongue tasted the wine, that, too, turned into solid gold.

'Bring me food!' he commanded.

His cooks brought their choicest dishes and set them before him. But when the meat and the bread reached his mouth, they became gold, as hard as stone. He took a peach from the golden salver, and it lay heavy and cold in his hand.

'Alas! I have been a fool! I have asked for the Golden Touch, and now, even though I am the richest man in the world, I must die of hunger and thirst!' said Midas.

He called out to the god, Dionysus. He said, 'Great god! You were right and I was wrong. Forgive me! Take back your gift!'

Dionysus laughed. But he was sorry for King Midas. He told him, 'Go and wash in the river and you will be free from the Golden Touch. Then everything that has changed will become itself again.'

The trees swayed in the wind. The flowers smelled sweet. Midas ate a huge meal. He enjoyed the red wine and the good bread.

He was very happy now, even though he was no longer the richest man in the world.

This story is a retelling of the Greek myth by Catherine Storr.

Knurremurre

There was once a little dwarf man called
Katto, and there was once a little dwarf
woman called Ulva; and like many a pair
of little dwarfs before and after them,
Katto and Ulva fell in love with one
another. They should have been happy,
and they could have been happy, had it
not been for Knurremurre. They should
have got married, and they would have
got married, had it not been that this same
Knurremurre fancied the little dwarf
woman for himself. And Knurremurre
was a terror!

Of all the dwarfs that lived under the

hill, he was the strongest; and of all the
dwarfs that lived under the hill, he was
the richest and the fiercest and the most
ill-tempered. In fact, he was a horrible
little fellow, and all the other dwarfs were
afraid of him.

So when Knurremurre said he was
going to marry Ulva himself, what could
poor Katto do but bow his head and hide
his grief? And what could poor Ulva do?
True, she didn't bow her head and hide
her grief: she clung to Katto, and threw

back her head, and howled long and loud. But that didn't do her any good. Knurre-murre seized her by the hair and dragged her away from Katto, and he got an iron ring and pushed it on to her finger, and called all the dwarfs together to witness the marriage ceremony.

'So now you are mine!' he snarled at poor Ulva. 'And don't you ever forget it!'

Katto felt that he couldn't stay there under the hill, looking forever at Ulva with longing eyes, and have Ulva forever looking with longing eyes at him. He thought it would be better for them both if he went away. So he changed himself into a fine tortoiseshell cat – perhaps it was his name that gave him the cat idea; at any rate he was a very special-looking cat, with a handsome coat and the most beautiful brown and yellow markings: a cat that any one would be proud to possess. So he thought he would have no difficulty in finding a good home.

And he did find a good home. He went

and rubbed himself against the door post of a house belonging to a man called Plat. Plat and his wife were delighted to see him, and they took him in and buttered his paws and gave him a dish of cream. And then he sat in a warm armchair by the stove and purred.

Well, if he could have forgotten Ulva he would have been happy. He had milk and he had bread and he had meat, and he wasn't expected to do anything except look handsome and catch a few mice when he felt inclined. But he couldn't forget Ulva; and so, though he wasn't exactly unhappy, he wasn't exactly happy.

And he lived like that for quite a long time.

Then one morning early, Mr Plat set out for market. There was nothing un-usual about that, because Mr Plat always had set out for market every Wednesday of his married life. He always set off at eight o'clock in the morning, and he always came back at six o'clock in the evening. And on the Wednesday I'm telling of, he did just that: except that the old clock over the dresser said maybe a few minutes past six when he walked in.

His wife set his supper on the table, and put a saucer of milk on the floor; and Plat sat down at the table, and the tortoiseshell cat jumped out of the armchair, and gave a stretch to his front legs and a stretch to his back legs. And then he settled himself to lap up the milk in his dainty way.

Plat ate a few mouthfuls, and then he put down his knife and fork and laughed.

'I've had a bit of an adventure this evening, that I have,' he said.

'Tell about it,' said his wife.

And the tortoiseshell cat went on lapping up the milk.

'You ever seen a dwarf?' said Plat.

'No, nor wish to,' said his wife.

The tortoiseshell cat stopped lapping the milk for a moment, and lifted up his green eyes to Plat.

114

'Nor I haven't seen one, neither,' said Plat.

'Then why speak of them?' said the wife.

And the tortoiseshell cat went on lapping up the milk.

'I'm coming to that,' said Plat. 'Now listen, old woman. I was walking across the moor, pleasant as you please, and as I came by a bit of a hill, something hit me on the knee.'

'That would be a pebble you kicked up,' said the wife.

And the tortoiseshell cat went on lapping up the milk.

'No, it wasn't a pebble I kicked up,' said Plat. 'It was a pebble thrown at me.'

'No, not *thrown* at you!' said the wife.

'Yes, thrown at me,' said Plat.

And the tortoiseshell cat went on lapping up the milk.

'Who threw it?' said the wife.

'I'm coming to that,' said Plat.

'Well then, come to it!' said the wife.

'So I stopped for to rub my knee,' said Plat. 'And I heard a squeak, squeak, squeaking.'

'That would be a bat flickering by in the air,' said the wife.

And the tortoiseshell cat went on lapping up the milk.

'No, it wasn't a bat flickering by in the air,' said Plat. 'It was a voice coming up from the ground.'

'No, not a *voice*!' said the wife.

'Yes, a voice,' said Plat.

And the tortoiseshell cat lifted his chin from the milk and stared at Plat out of his great green eyes.

'A little bit of a squeaky voice,' said Plat, 'and it was speaking words.'

'No, not *words*!' said the wife.

'Yes, words,' said Plat. 'I heard 'em plain.'

The tortoiseshell cat was still staring at Plat, and Plat stared back and said, 'Seems like our puss is listening.'

'No, our puss isn't listening,' said the

wife. 'Tell what the voice said; if it was a voice, which I'm not believing.'

'It was a voice,' said Plat, 'and this is what it said:

> *Hark'ee, Plat,*
> *Tell your cat*
> *That Knurremurre's dead.*

Now why should I go for to tell our cat a thing the like of that?'

'It doesn't make sense,' said the wife.

It didn't make sense to them, but it made sense to the cat. He jumped up in such a hurry that he overset the saucer of milk. Then he stood on his hind legs and clapped his paws in the air.

'What! Is Knurremurre dead?' he cried in a shrill voice. 'Then I may go home as fast as I please!'

And he began to dance round the room and sing,

'Knurremurre is dead! Knurremurre is dead!
So I thank you for board and I thank you for
> *bed,*
And Katto and Ulva this night shall be wed.'

And with that he gave a leap through the window, and galloped off towards the dwarfs' hill, with his tail sticking up like a flag pole.

Plat stared at his wife, and his wife stared at him.

'Did you ever?' said Plat.

'No, I never did,' said the wife.

This story is a retelling of the traditional tale by Ruth Manning-Sanders.

The Nightingale

You know, of course, that in China the emperor is Chinese, and so are all of his people. The story that I'm going to tell you happened many years ago, and that is why you should hear it now before it is forgotten.

The emperor's palace was the finest in the world. It was made entirely of delicate porcelain that was so precious and fragile that you had to be tremendously careful how you touched anything. The garden was full of rare flowers, and the loveliest of these had little silver bells tied to them, and they tinkled whenever anyone passed.

Yes, everything in the emperor's garden was arranged most carefully, and it stretched so far that even the gardener had no idea where it ended. If you kept walking, you came to a glorious wood with tall trees and deep lakes. The wood went down to the sea, which was blue and very deep — deep enough for ships to sail in under the branches of the trees. In the wood lived a nightingale that sang enchantingly. A poor fisherman, who had so much to do each evening, always paused to listen while pulling in his nets. 'That's lovely!' he praised, then went on with his work and soon forgot the bird. Yet when he sang the following night the fisherman briefly stopped work again. 'My word,' he repeated, 'that is lovely!'

From every country in the world travellers came to marvel at the emperor's city, his palace and garden; but as soon as the nightingale sang they declared that his song was even more remarkable. All returned home with tales to tell, and some

120

wrote books about the city, the palace and the garden, but the nightingale was given place of honour. And poets wrote long verses about the nightingale in the wood that was beside the deep sea.

These books were read by the world, and so in the course of time, some of them reached the emperor. He sat in his golden chair, reading and reading. Now and then his head nodded to show his pleasure in the splendid descriptions of the city, the palace and the garden. Then he came across a sentence that read, 'But the song of the nightingale is the most amazing of all.'

'What's this?' thought the emperor. 'The nightingale! What nightingale? I've never heard of him. Is there such a bird in my empire, here in my garden? Nobody ever told me. One must read about it in a book.' And, with that, he summoned his gentleman-in-waiting, who was so grand that, whenever anyone of lower rank tried to speak to him or ask a question, he only answered, 'Ph!' And that didn't mean anything at all.

'It says here that we have a most remarkable bird called a nightingale,' began the emperor. 'It says here that there's nothing to equal him in the empire. Why haven't I heard of him before?'

'I command him to be brought here this evening to sing to me,' instructed the emperor. 'All the world knows of him, yet I know nothing.'

'It's the first I've ever heard of him,' repeated the gentleman-in-waiting. 'I shall look for him, and I shall find him.'

Find him? But where? The gentleman-in-waiting ran upstairs then downstairs, through rooms and passages, but none of the people he met had heard of the nightingale. So, the gentleman-in-waiting hurried once more to the emperor to declare that the nightingale was an invention by those who had written the books. 'Your Majesty must not believe everything that you read. Most of it is made up. It's fiction. Just stories.'

'But I've just read the book that was sent to me by the High and Mighty Emperor of Japan,' replied the emperor. 'Therefore every word of it must be true. I *will* hear the nightingale. He will come and sing tonight. If he fails to appear, then every courtier shall be thumped in the stomach directly after supper.'

'Tsing-pe!' spluttered the gentleman-in-waiting. He ran up and down the stairs again, through all the rooms and passages again, with half the court running behind him. None of them wanted to be thumped in the stomach so they asked everywhere for the extraordinary nightingale that everybody knew about except the people at court.

Finally, a little girl scrubbing pots and pans in the kitchen answered. 'That nightingale? Yes, I know him well. And he can sing,' she remembered. 'Every evening

I'm allowed to take home some leftovers to my sick mother who lives by the shore. On my way back I often rest in the wood, and I hear the nightingale singing. It brings tears to my eyes as if my mother were kissing me.'

'Kitchen-maid,' said the gentleman-in-waiting, 'I shall arrange a kitchen promotion for you. You shall be allowed to watch the emperor eat his dinner, but only if you'll take us to the nightingale. He's to give a command performance this evening before the emperor.'

So half the court escorted the gentleman-in-waiting and the kitchen-maid on the quest. As they walked a cow began lowing. 'Ah, there he is!' cried out the courtiers. 'What a remarkable voice for such a small creature! Even so, it's not the first time we've heard him.'

'That's a cow mooing,' said the little kitchen-maid. 'We've still a long way to go.'

Then frogs creaked in a pond. 'Delightful!' enthused the emperor's chaplain. 'Can you hear him? A voice that rings like church bells.'

'No, no. They are frogs,' explained the little kitchen-maid. 'But we may hear him very soon.'

Just then the nightingale burst into song.

'There he is,' whispered the little girl. 'Listen, oh, do listen! There he is, up there . . .' and she pointed to a little grey bird in the branches.

'Is it possible?' bleated the gentleman-in-waiting. 'I never pictured him looking like that. How ordinary he is! Perhaps he's lost his colour because he's embarrassed to see so many distinguished persons about him.'

'Little nightingale,' called out the kitchen-maid. 'Our gracious emperor wants you to sing to him.'

'I shall with the greatest of pleasure,'

answered the nightingale, and began to sing delightfully.

'Oh, his voice! It's just like tinkling bells,' observed the gentleman-in-waiting. 'How his throat keeps throbbing. I can't make out why we've never heard him before. He'll be a great success at court.'

'Shall I sing once more for the emperor?' asked the nightingale who believed that the emperor was there.

'Excellent little nightingale,' began the gentleman-in-waiting, 'it is my pleasant duty to invite you to court this evening where you will enchant His Imperial Majesty with your exquisite singing.'

'But my voice sounds best here, in the wood,' said the nightingale, but, since it was the emperor's wish, he readily agreed to sing at court.

The palace had been polished until the glittering china walls and floors reflected, like mirrors, the light of thousands and thousands of gold lamps. Everywhere were arrangements of the loveliest flowers, the ones with silver bells. The draughts created by scurrying servants caused the bells to tinkle so loudly that you wouldn't have heard a word that was spoken.

In the middle of the great hall stood the emperor's throne with a golden perch for the nightingale beside it. The entire court, all dressed in their finest clothes, were present; and the kitchen-maid, who now ranked as Imperial Kitchen-Maid, was allowed to stand behind the door to listen and even peep at the little grey bird.

The emperor nodded for the nightingale to begin his song. It was of such beauty, tears stung the emperor's eyes, then trickled down his cheeks. The songs grew even lovelier and went straight to the emperor's heart, and he ordered his most esteemed award, the Golden Slipper, to be hung about the nightingale's neck.

'No, thank you,' said the nightingale.

'I've seen tears in the eyes of the emperor and that's my richest reward. There's a strange power in an emperor's tears. Heaven knows that they are reward enough.' Then the nightingale sang again.

'Whoever heard a more elegant voice,' murmured the court ladies, and later, believing that they too could sound like the nightingale, filled their mouths with water so as to gurgle when anyone spoke to them. Even the lackeys and the ladies' maids expressed their approval and that's saying a great deal, because they are the most difficult people to satisfy. There was no doubt whatever, the nightingale was a success.

He was now to remain at court in his own cage, with permission to walk twice daily and once at night. Twelve servants attended him, each one tightly holding a silken ribbon fastened to his leg. There was absolutely no fun in such a walk.

Soon the whole city talked of the remarkable bird. When two people met,

129

one of them said, 'Night!' and the other merely answered, 'Gale!' and they perfectly understood each other. Then, twelve grocer's children were named after him, but not one of them could sing a note.

One day a large parcel, with *Nightingale* written on it, arrived for the emperor. 'I expect this is a new book about our famous bird,' said the emperor. It wasn't a book at all. It was a mechanical bird lying in the box. It was supposed to look like a live nightingale but it was studded with diamonds, rubies and sapphires. You only had to wind it up and it sang one of the real nightingale's songs, while fluttering its little tail that glittered with silver and gold. Written on a ribbon that hung around its neck, was, 'The Emperor of Japan's nightingale is inferior to the Emperor of China's.'

'How delightful!' exclaimed the court. And the messenger who delivered the bird was given the title 'Supreme Imperial Nightingale Deliverer'.

'Perhaps they could sing together,' someone suggested. 'It would be a duet.'

The two birds did sing together, but it was not successful because the true nightingale sang in his own natural way, while the artificial nightingale trilled mechanically. 'Of course, it can't be blamed for that,' said the Master of the Emperor's Music. 'It keeps perfect time and follows my teaching methods exactly.'

After that the artificial bird sang alone and immediately they all thought it equal to the live bird. Besides, it was much prettier, sparkling there like a cluster of bejewelled brooches and bracelets. So, over and over, thirty-three times the mechanical bird sang its song without growing tired. The court longed to hear it once more, but the emperor thought it was now time for the true nightingale to sing . . . But where was he? No-one had noticed him fly through an open window, back to his green wood.

'Bless my soul, what is the meaning of this?' demanded the emperor, and the court indignantly accused the bird of being an ungrateful creature.

'Still, the best bird is here,' they reminded him and were enchanted to hear the artificial bird sing the same song for the thirty-fourth time.

Even so, no-one had quite learnt the difficult melody, and the bird earned extraordinary praise from the Music Master. In fact, he declared that it was superior to the nightingale, not merely because of its outward glittering appearance of wonderful jewels, but also for its mechanical insides. 'You see, Your Imperial Majesty, ladies and gentlemen, we could not depend upon the live bird. There's no telling what he'd sing. But with the artificial bird, the song is fixed beforehand. That song and no other will be heard,' he explained. 'We can examine the bird's works and admire the human mind that invented the wheels and cylinders, putting them into position so that they work precisely.'

Everyone agreed with the Music Master who asked for imperial permission to display the bird to the public on the following Sunday. 'Yes, they must also hear it sing,' nodded the emperor. And hear it they did. People were delighted as if they had drunk themselves merry on tea – that's so very Chinese! 'Oh!' they said, nodding their heads and holding up one finger, the finger we call Lickpot. 'Yes, it doesn't sound too bad,' said the fisherman who had heard the real bird in the wood, 'and yet there's something missing, but I don't know what.'

The true nightingale was sent into exile, banished from the realm. The artificial bird rested on a silk cushion, close to the emperor's bed. All the presents it had received, including gold and precious stones, were piled about it. Then it was promoted to Grand Imperial Bedside Minstrel, with the rank of First Class on the Left, because the emperor considered the side on which the heart lies to be the more distinguished, as even the emperor's heart is placed on the left.

The Master of Music wrote a long and learned book of twenty-five volumes about the mechanical bird. It was packed with long and difficult Chinese words, and everyone pretended that they had both read it and understood it, otherwise they would have been thought stupid and thumped in the stomach.

A whole year passed. The emperor, his court and the Chinese people knew by heart every trill from the throat of the Grand Imperial Bedside Minstrel, and for that very reason they liked the artificial songbird so much and joined in its song. 'Zee-zee-zee, kloo-kloo-klook!' the street boys sang. 'Zee-zee-zee, kloo-kloo-klook!' the emperor sang. 'Zee-zee-zee, kloo-kloo-klook!' everybody sang.

One evening, while the emperor lay in bed listening as the mechanical bird sang at its peak, something went, 'snap!' A whirr sounded inside the bird. Wheels whizzed . . . and the music stopped.

Quickly the emperor jumped out of bed and sent for the doctor. But what could he do? So the emperor sent for the Imperial Watchmaker, and after a great deal of talk and poking about, he repaired the bird so that it worked after a fashion, but he warned that it must not be used too often. The bearings were almost worn out and it was impossible to get new parts that would suit the clockwork. This was a sad disappointment. Only yearly, now, was the artificial bird allowed to sing, and on these occasions the Master of Music made a little speech, using difficult words, to explain that the bird was as good as ever.

Five years passed, and by then the kingdom was filled with sorrow. Their emperor was so ill it was thought that he was unlikely to live, and they were fond of him. A new emperor had already been chosen, and people stood in the street to ask the gentleman-in-waiting about their beloved emperor. 'Ph!' he replied, shaking his head.

Cold and pale lay the emperor in his magnificent golden bed. The whole court believed him to be dead, and each of them hurried off to pay their respects to the new emperor. The valets flocked to the street, full of gossip, and the palace house-maids had a large tea-party. Everywhere, in every room and hall, heavy cloth had been laid to silence the sound of footsteps and the whole palace was still and quiet.

But the emperor was not dead yet. Through an open window high in a wall, the moon shone down on the emperor and the artificial nightingale. He lay pale and motionless, his bed decorated with long velvet curtains, trimmed with heavy tassels of gold silk.

The emperor could hardly breathe. It was as if something sat on his chest. He opened his eyes and saw it was Death sitting there, wearing his own gold crown and holding his golden sword in one hand and the imperial standard in the other. About the bed, from the folds in the velvet curtains, strange faces peered at the emperor — hideous faces, frightening faces, gentle and kind faces — the faces of his good and evil deeds. They stared down at him while Death sat on his heart. 'Do you remember this?' they whispered, one after the other. 'Do you remember?' they asked and told him so much about his past life that the sweat stood out on his forehead.

'No, no, I remember nothing,' cried out the emperor. 'Music! Music! Bring me the sound of the great Chinese drum,' he begged. 'Save me from hearing what they say.'

But the faces kept talking, and Death, in the Chinese way, nodded his head to every word.

'Sing, little golden nightingale!' demanded the emperor. 'I have given you gold

137

and precious stones and I have hung my golden slipper around your neck with my own hands. Sing! Please, sing!'

But the artificial bird stayed silent. No-one came to wind it, so it could not sing. And Death, with huge hollow eyes, went on staring silently at the emperor. Everything was still, so terribly still.

All at once, by the window, came a burst of most wonderful singing. It was the little nightingale perched in a tree outside and he sang of comfort and hope to ease the emperor's distress. The bird had flown to him immediately upon hearing of his illness and his voice filled the imperial bedroom, while the faces in the curtains faded, growing fainter and fainter, while the blood pulsed faster and faster through the emperor's weak limbs. Death himself listened and said, 'Go on, little nightingale. Go on singing.'

'I will sing on if you'll give me the fine gold sword,' he promised. 'And if you'll

138

give me the imperial banner . . . and if you'll give me the emperor's crown.'

Death willingly gave up each treasure for a song, and still the nightingale sang. He sang of the quiet churchyard where the white roses bloom, where the elderberry is fragrant and where the fresh grass is watered with the tears of those who come to mourn. Death longed for this garden and floated like a cold white mist through the window.

'Thank you, thank you!' whispered the emperor. 'You heavenly little bird, I remember you. I banished you from the kingdom, and yet you returned to banish in turn the evil visions from my bed and lift Death from my heart. How can I ever reward you?'

'You have done so,' replied the nightingale. 'I have not forgotten that my song once brought tears to your eyes. Such tears are jewels that bring joy to a singer's heart. But you must sleep to grow well and strong again. I will sing to you.' And during his song the emperor fell into a healing sleep, a peaceful refreshing sleep.

He awoke restored. The sun shone through the windows. The nightingale still sang softly, outside the window, but no servant had entered. They thought he was dead.

'Don't leave me again,' begged the emperor. 'You shall sing only when you wish. I shall break the artificial bird into a thousand pieces.'

'No, don't do that,' said the nightingale. 'It's done what it could. Don't part with it yet. I can't make my home in the palace but I shall visit you often,' he promised. 'Each evening I'll sit on the branch by your window, and my songs will make you both happy and thoughtful. I shall sing of those who are contented and of those who suffer. I shall sing of the good and evil that happens in your kingdom but is hidden from you. A songbird flies far and I can visit the huts of fishermen and peasants — all your people who live away from you and your court. Emperor, I love your heart better than your crown, yet there is the breath of something holy about the crown. Yes, I shall come. I shall sing. One thing only do I ask of you.'

'I'll grant you anything,' answered the emperor, standing now in his imperial robes that he himself had put on, and he held his heavy sword before his heart.

'I beg you to let no-one know that you have a little bird who tells you everything. That will be best,' said the nightingale and flew away.

Then servants crept into the royal chamber to look upon their dead Emperor, and they stood there gaping when he said, 'Good morning!'

This is a retelling, by Jean Chapman, of Hans Andersen's original story.

141

Ramona the Brave

Filled with spirit and pluck, Ramona started off to school with her lunch box in her hand. She was determined that today would be different. She would make it different. She was her father's spunky gal, wasn't she? She twirled around for the pleasure of making her pleated skirt stand out beneath her car coat.

Ramona was so filled with spunk she decided to go to school a different way, by the next street over, something she had always wanted to do. The distance to Glenwood School was no greater. There was no reason she should not go to school any way she pleased as long as she looked both ways before she crossed the street and did not talk to strangers.

Slowpoke Howie, half a block behind, called out when he saw her turn the corner, 'Ramona, where are you going?'

'I'm going to school a different way,' Ramona called back, certain that Howie would not follow to spoil her feeling of adventure. Howie was not a boy to change his ways.

Ramona skipped happily down the street, singing to herself, 'Hippity-hop to the barber shop to buy a stick of candy. One for you and one for me and one for sister Mandy.' The sky through the bare branches overhead was clear, the air was crisp, and Ramona's feet in their brown oxfords felt light. Beezus's old boots, which so often weighed her down, were home in the hall closet. Ramona was happy. The day felt different already.

Ramona turned the second corner, and as she hippity-hopped down the unfamiliar street past three white houses and a tan stucco house, she enjoyed a feeling of freedom and adventure. Then as she passed a grey shingle house in the middle of the block, a large German shepherd dog, licence tags jingling, darted down the driveway towards her. Terrified, Ramona stood rooted to the sidewalk. She felt as if her bad dreams had come true. The grass was green, the sky was blue. She could not move; she could not scream.

The dog, head thrust forward, came close. He sniffed with his black nose. Here was a stranger. He growled. This was his territory, and he did not want a stranger to trespass.

This is not a dream, Ramona told herself. This is real. My feet will move if I make them. 'Go 'way!' she ordered, backing away from the dog, which answered with a sharp bark. He had teeth like the wolf in *Little Red Riding Hood*. Oh, Grandmother, what big teeth you have! The better to eat you with, my dear.

144

Ramona took another step back. Growling, the dog advanced. He was a dog, not a wolf, but that was bad enough.

Ramona used the only weapon she had – her lunch box. She slung her lunch box at the dog and missed. The box crashed to the sidewalk, tumbled, and came to rest.

The dog stopped to sniff it. Ramona forced her feet to move, to run. Her oxfords pounded on the sidewalk. One shoelace came untied and slapped against her ankle. She looked desperately at a passing car, but the driver did not notice her peril.

Ramona cast a terrified look over her shoulder. The dog had lost interest in her unopened lunch box and was coming towards her again. She could hear his toenails on the sidewalk and could hear him growling deep in his throat. She had to do something, but what?

Ramona's heart was pounding in her ears as she stopped to reach for the only weapon left — her shoe. She had no choice. She yanked off her brown oxford and hurled it at the dog. Again she missed. The dog stopped, sniffed the shoe, and then to Ramona's horror, picked it up, and trotted off in the direction from which he had come.

Ramona stood aghast with the cold

from the concrete sidewalk seeping through her sock. Now what should she do? If she said, You come back here, the dog might obey, and she did not want him any closer. She watched helplessly as he returned to his own lawn, where he settled down with the shoe between his paws like a bone. He began to gnaw.

Her shoe! There was no way Ramona could take her shoe away from the dog by herself. There was no-one she could ask for help on this street of strangers. And her blue lunch box, now dented, lying there on the sidewalk. Did she dare try to get it back while the dog was busy chewing her shoe? She took a cautious step towards her lunch box. The dog went on gnawing. She took another step. I really am brave, she told herself. The dog looked up. Ramona froze. The dog began to gnaw again. She darted forward, grabbed her lunch box, and ran towards school, *slap-pat, slap-pat*, on the cold concrete.

Ramona refused to cry — she was brave, wasn't she? — but she was worried. Mrs Griggs frowned on tardiness, and Ramona was quite sure she expected everyone in her class to wear two shoes. Ramona would probably catch it from Mrs Griggs at school and from her mother at home for losing a shoe with a lot of wear left in it. Ramona was always catching it.

When Ramona reached Glenwood School, the bell had rung and the traffic boys were leaving their posts. The children crowding into the building did not notice Ramona's predicament. Ramona *slap-patted* down the hall to Room One, where she quickly left her lunch box and car coat in the cloakroom before she sat down at her desk with one foot folded under her. She spread her pleated skirt to hide her dirty sock.

Susan noticed. 'What happened to your other shoe?' she asked.

'I lost it, and don't you tell!' If Susan

told, Ramona would have a good excuse to pull Susan's *boing-boing* curls.

'I won't,' promised Susan, pleased to share a secret, 'but how are you going to keep Mrs Griggs from finding out?'

Ramona cast a desperate look at Susan. 'I don't know,' she confessed.

'Class,' said Mrs Griggs in a calm voice. This was her way of saying, All right, everyone quiet down and come to order because we have work to do, and we won't accomplish anything if we waste time talking to one another. Ramona tried to warm her cold foot by rubbing it through her pleated skirt.

Mrs Griggs looked around her classroom. 'Who has not had a turn at leading the flag salute?' she asked.

Ramona stared at her desk while trying to shrink so small Mrs Griggs could not see her.

'Ramona, you have not had a turn,' said Mrs Griggs with a smile. 'You may come to the front of the room.'

149

Ramona and Susan exchanged a look. Ramona's said, Now what am I going to do? Susan's said, I feel sorry for you.

'Ramona, we're waiting,' said Mrs Griggs.

There was no escape. Ramona slid from her seat and walked to the front of the room where she faced the flag and stood on one foot like a stork to hide her shoeless foot behind her pleated skirt. 'I pledge allegiance,' she began, swaying.

'I pledge allegiance,' said the class.

Mrs Griggs interrupted. 'Both feet on the floor, Ramona.'

Ramona felt a surge of defiance. Mrs Griggs wanted two feet on the floor, so she put two feet on the floor, '— to the flag,' she continued with such determination that Mrs Griggs did not have another chance to interrupt. When Ramona finished, she took her seat. So there, Mrs Griggs, was her spunky thought. What if I am wearing only one shoe?

'Ramona, what happened to your other shoe?' asked Mrs Griggs.

'I lost it,' answered Ramona.

'Tell me about it,' said Mrs Griggs.

Ramona did not want to tell. 'I was chased by a . . .' She wanted to say gorilla, but after a moment's hesitation she said, '. . . dog, and I had to throw my shoe at him, and he ran off with it.'

She expected the class to laugh, but instead they listened in silent sympathy. They did not understand about a hole in a house, but they understood about big dogs. They too had faced big dogs and been frightened. Ramona felt better.

'Why, that's too bad,' said Mrs Griggs, which surprised Ramona. Somehow she had not expected her teacher to understand. Mrs Griggs continued. 'I'll call the office and ask the secretary to telephone your mother and have her bring you another pair of shoes.'

'My mother isn't home,' said Ramona. 'She's at work.'

'Well, don't worry, Ramona,' said Mrs Griggs. 'We have some boots without owners in the cloakroom. You may borrow one to wear when we go out for recess.'

Ramona was familiar with those boots, none of them related and all of them a dingy brown, because no-one would lose a new red boot. If there was one thing Ramona did not like, it was old brown boots. They were really ugly. She could not run and play kickball in one shoe and one boot. Spirit and spunk surged back

152

into Ramona. Mrs Griggs meant well, but she did not understand about boots. Miss Binney would never have told Ramona to wear one old boot. Ramona did not want to wear an old brown boot, and she made up her mind she was not going to wear an old brown boot!

Once Ramona had made this decision, it was up to her to decide what to do about it. If only she had some heavy paper and a stapler, she could make a slipper, one that might even be strong enough to last until she reached home. She paid attention to number combinations in one part of her mind, while in that private place in the back of her mind she thought about a paper slipper and how she could make one if only she had a stapler. A stapler, a stapler, where could she find a stapler? Mrs Griggs would want an explanation if she asked to borrow Room One's stapler. To borrow Miss Binney's stapler, Ramona would have to run across the playground to the temporary building, and Mrs Griggs was sure to call her back. There had to be another way. And there was, if only she could make it work.

When recess finally came, Ramona was careful to leave the room with several other members of her class and to slip down to the girls' cloakroom in the basement before Mrs Griggs could remind her to put on the boot. She jerked four rough paper towels out of the container by the sinks. She folded three of the paper towels in half, making six layers of rough paper. The fourth towel she folded in thirds, which also made six layers of paper.

Now came the scary part of her plan, Ramona returned to the hall, which was empty because both first grades were out on the playground. The doors of the classrooms were closed. No-one would see the brave thing she was about to do. Ramona climbed the stairs to the first landing, where she paused to take a fresh grip on her courage. She had never gone to the upstairs hall alone. First graders rarely ventured there unless accompanied by their parents on Open House night. She felt small and frightened, but she held fast to her courage, as she ran up the second half of the flight of stairs.

Ramona found Mr Cardoza's room. She quietly opened the door a crack. Mr Cardoza was telling his class, 'Spelling *secretary* is easy. Just remember the first part of the word is *secret* and think of a *secretary* as someone who keeps *secrets*. You will never again spell the word with two *a*'s instead of two *e*'s.'

Ramona opened the door a little wider and peeped inside. How big the desks looked compared to her own down in Room One! She heard the whir of a wheel spinning in a mouse's cage.

Mr Cardoza came to investigate. He opened the door wider and said, 'Hello, Ramona Q. What may we do for you?'

There was Ramona standing on one foot, trying to hide her dirty sock behind her shoe while Beezus's whole class, and especially Beezus, stared at her. Beside her classmates Beezus did not look so big as Ramona had always thought her to be. Ramona was secretly pleased to discover her sister was a little less than medium-sized. Ramona wondered how Beezus would report this scene at home. Mother! The door opened, and there was Ramona standing with one shoe on . . .

Ramona refused to let her courage fail her. She remembered her manners and asked, 'May I please borrow your stapler? I can use it right here in the hall, and it will only take a minute.'

Once again she had that strange feeling of standing aside to look at herself. Was she a funny little girl whom Mr Cardoza would find amusing? Apparently not because Mr Cardoza did not hesitate.

'Certainly,' he said and strode to his desk for the stapler, which he handed to her without question. Mrs Griggs would have said, Tell me why you want it, Ramona. Miss Binney would have said,

Won't you let me help you with it? Mr Cardoza closed the door, leaving Ramona in the privacy of the hall.

Ramona knelt on the floor and went to work. She stapled the three paper towels together. The towel folded in thirds she placed at one end of the other towels and stapled it on three sides to make the toe of a slipper. She had to push down hard with both hands to force the staples through so much paper. Then she turned her slipper over and sent staples through in the other direction to make it stronger. There. Ramona slid her foot into her slipper. With more time and a pair of scissors, she could have made a better slipper with a rounded toe, but this slipper was better than an old boot, and it should last all day, school paper towels being what they were.

Ramona opened the door again and held out the stapler. Mr Cardoza looked up from the book in his hand and walked over to take the stapler from her. 'Thank you, Mr Cardoza,' she said, because she knew he expected good manners.

'You're welcome, Ramona Q,' said Mr Cardoza with a smile that was a friendly smile, not an amused-by-a-funny-little-girl smile. 'We're always glad to be of help.'

Ramona had not felt so happy since she was in Miss Binney's kindergarten. Too bad Beezus had first dibs on Mr Cardoza. Ramona might have married him herself some day if she ever decided to get married. She reached Room One just as the two first grades were returning from recess. She heard someone from Room Two say, 'Ramona must have hurt her foot.'

Someone else said, 'I bet it hurts.'

Ramona began to limp. She was enjoying the attention her slipper attracted.

'Oh, there you are, Ramona,' said Mrs Griggs, who was standing by her door to make sure her class entered the room in an orderly manner. 'Where have you been?

We missed you on the playground.'

'I was making a slipper.' Ramona looked up at Mrs Griggs. 'I didn't want to wear a dirty old boot.' She had not felt so brave since the day she started off to the first grade.

'After this you should ask permission to stay in during recess.' Mrs Griggs looked down at the slipper and said, 'You have made a very good slipper.'

Encouraged by this bit of praise, Ramona said, 'I could make a better slipper if I had scissors and crayons. I could draw a bunny face on the toe and make ears like a real bunny slipper.'

Mrs Griggs's expression was thoughtful. She seemed to be studying Ramona, who shrank inside herself, uncertain as to what her teacher might be about to say. Mrs Griggs looked more tired than cross, so Ramona summoned her spunk and said, 'Maybe I could finish my slipper instead of making a Thanksgiving turkey.'

'We always — ' began Mrs Griggs and changed her mind. 'I don't see why not,' she said.

Mrs Griggs approved of her! Ramona smiled with relief and pretended to limp to her seat as her teacher closed the door. She no longer had to dread turkeys — or her teacher.

The class took out arithmetic workbooks. While Ramona began to count cowboy boots and butterflies and circled the correct number under the pictures, she was busy and happy in the private corner of her mind planning improvements in her slipper. She would round the heel and toe. She would draw a nose with pink crayon and eyes, too, and cut two ears . . . Ramona's happy thoughts were interrupted by another less happy thought. Her missing brown oxford. What was her mother going to say when she came home without it? Tell her she was careless? Tell her how much shoes cost these days? Ask her why on earth she didn't go to school the usual way? Because I was feeling full of spunk, Ramona answered in her thoughts. Her father would understand. She hoped her mother would, too.

Workbooks were collected. Reading circles were next. Prepared to attack words, Ramona limped to a little chair in the front of the room with the rest of her reading group. She felt so much better towards Mrs Griggs that she was first to raise her hand on almost every question, even though she was worried about her missing oxford. The reader was more interesting now that her group was attacking bigger words. *Fire engine.* Ramona read to herself and thought, Pow! I got you, *fire engine. Monkey.* Pow! I got you, *monkey.*

The buzz of the little black telephone beside Mrs Griggs's desk interrupted work in Room One. Everyone wanted to listen to Mrs Griggs talk to the principal's office, because they might hear something important.

'Yes,' said Mrs Griggs to the telephone. 'Yes, we do.' With the receiver pressed to her ear, she turned away from the telephone and looked at Ramona. Everyone else in Room One looked at her, too. Now what? thought Ramona. Now what have I done? 'All right,' said Mrs Griggs to the telephone. 'I'll send her along.' She replaced the receiver. Room One, most of all Ramona, waited.

'Ramona, your shoe is waiting for you in the office,' said the teacher. 'When the dog's owner found it on the lawn, he brought it to school and the secretary guessed it was a first-grade size. You may be excused to go get it.'

Whew! thought Ramona in great relief, as she limped happily off to the office. This day was turning out to be better than she had expected. She accepted her shoe, now interestingly scarred with toothmarks, from Mrs Miller, the school secretary.

'My goodness,' said Mrs Miller, as

Ramona shoved her foot into her shoe and tied the lace, still damp from being chewed, in a tight bow. 'It's a good thing your foot came out of your shoe when the dog got hold of it. He must have had pretty big teeth.'

'He did,' Ramona assured the secretary. 'Great big teeth. Like a wolf. He chased me.' Now that Ramona was safe in her two shoes, she was eager for an audience. 'He chased me, but I took off my shoe and threw it at him, and that stopped him.'

'Fancy that!' Mrs Miller was plainly impressed by Ramona's story. 'You took off your shoe and threw it right at him! You must be a very brave girl.'

'I guess maybe I am,' said Ramona, pleased by the compliment. Of course, she was brave. She had scars on her shoe to prove it. She hoped her mother would not be in too much of a hurry to hide the toothmarks with fresh shoe polish. She hippity-hopped, paper slipper in hand, down the hall to show off her scars to

Room One. Brave Ramona, that's what they would think, just about the bravest girl in the first grade. And they would be right. This time Ramona was sure.

This story is by Beverly Cleary.

The Three Hunters

Once there were three hunters; two were not dressed and the other had no clothes on.

And they had three guns; two were not loaded, and the other one was empty.

They left before daybreak and went far, far away — even farther than that.

Near a wood, they shot at three hares — *bang! bang! bang!* and missed two, while the third one ran away.

They put the two hares they had missed in the pocket of the hunter who had no clothes on.

'Goodness gracious!' they exclaimed. 'How shall we ever cook the hare that ran away?'

Then the three hunters started off

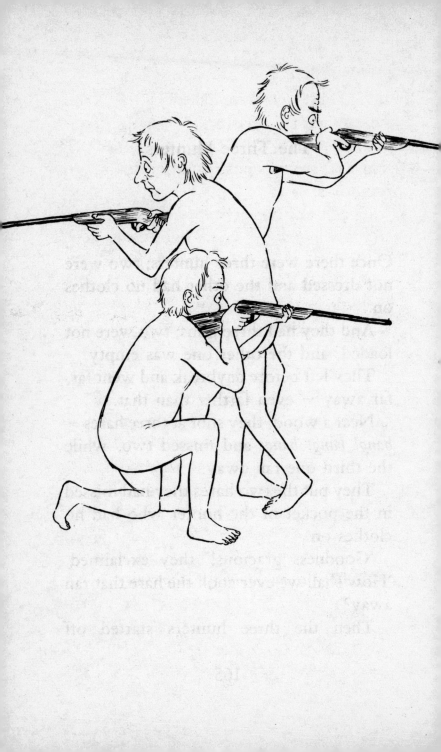

again. They went far, far away — but this time much farther than they hadn't gone before. At last they came to a house that had neither walls nor roof, nor doors, nor windows.

The three hunters rapped three times on the missing door, *knock! knock! knock!*

One who wasn't there answered: 'What is it? What do you want?'

'Please do us a favour. Lend us your skillet to cook the hare that got away from us.'

'Dearie me! gentlemen, we have only three skillets in the house, and two are broken and the third isn't any good!'

So the hunters sat down on the door-step that wasn't there, to decide what to do about it. And while they are thinking, let's finish this tale, as all stories must have an end.

This story is by Simone Chamoud.

The Wee Ghostie

Once there was a little girl-ghost who lived in the cupboard under the stairs, in an old house. She had lived there for many years, but she never got any older. Her pale little face kept its charming oval, her curved lips smiled and her eyes looked calmly down on the world her body had left long before.

She liked the little cupboard, where she dreamed and slept all day, only coming out at night when everyone was asleep. Then the planks in the cupboard floor squeaked, and the door rattled, and there was a sigh and a tiny moan as she slipped through a crack and walked in the house.

'It's only the ghostie,' explained the grandfather, who lived in the house with his daughter and her children. 'Take no notice of her and she won't take any notice of you. There's been a ghostie ever since I remember, but she's only a wee lassie.'

The children opened wide their eyes, but Judy, the youngest, sat very still, listening. She thought once that she heard a voice high and far away, crying, 'Oh-oh-oh, I can't find her. Oh-oh-oh.' It was like an owl calling in the trees, wailing and lost.

'The ghostie has lost something,' said Judy solemnly. 'She's lonely.'

'I dare say she has lost something,' answered her grandfather, 'but she lost it so long ago nobody can find it.'

'Let's turn out the cupboard and look,' said Judy. 'Then we can see the ghostie sleeping there.'

'You won't see her. She's invisible,'

said the grandfather. 'I don't think she sleeps there, she goes to a land in the air. But you can turn out the cupboard for it is in a mess. I can never find anything I want. Your mother will be glad to see it straightened.'

So the next wet day the three children turned out the deep cupboard under the stairs, and they found many things which might have been lost and might not. Old tennis racquets with strings broken, a cricket bat and stumps, a broken old basket, a heap of mildewed books with old-fashioned pictures, a folding chair, a child's cot, and some shoes, all lay under a pile of newspapers, and in them was a mouse's nest.

'That's the ghostie's house,' laughed Jane to Judy. 'That's what made the squeak and cry you heard.'

'I don't think so,' whispered Judy. 'It was a real voice, not an owl's or a mouse's.'

They carried the ball of feathers and

papers away and then returned to look at the empty cupboard. Nothing was left except dust and bits of plaster.

The hall was full of rubbish and Mother gasped when she saw it.

'What a terrible mess!' she cried. 'I had no idea we had so much stuff buried here.'

'We are looking for the ghostie,' explained Judy. 'And all we found was a mouse's nest, and this rubbish.'

'I used to think a ghostie lived here when I was little,' said her mother. 'I was shut here in the darkness when I was naughty, and I heard little moans and rustles.'

'Poor Mother,' said Judy. 'I'm glad you don't put us there. Were you very frightened?'

'No, I was rather afraid of the dark but I liked the little murmurs and the sounds. Now I never hear them. I had forgotten all about my little wee ghostie girl,' said her mother.

'Leave everything as it is,' she

continued. 'Miranda will scrub out the cupboard and make it all clean. Then I will sort out the things not worth keeping, and there will be much more room in this old cupboard.'

Miranda brought her brushes and her pail of hot water. She sighed at the dusky hole, and laughed at the tale of a ghostie, but she scrubbed and rubbed the boards and the walls, till the cupboard was clean as a new pin. One board was loose and when she put her pail on it, it squeaked and moaned.

'There's your ghostie,' she said to Judy who stood watching her. 'It wants a nail.'

She gave a tug of the loose board and it came away. A space was disclosed, and in it lay a little wooden box all smothered in cobwebs. She lifted it out and she saw the lid was held by a tiny brass latchet. She raised the latchet and the lid fell back on its brass hinges. Inside lay a small wooden doll, whose face was worn and rubbed with age. The black hair was painted on

its head, and its blue eyes looked out with astonishment from the small carved little face. The nose was nearly flat and the cheeks were pale pink. Curved red lips seemed to smile, as Miranda held up the doll for Judy to see. The white cotton dress sprigged with lilac was long and full, pleated and ruffled with tiny stitches, and its folds reached to the top of the black painted boots on the doll's legs. Round the doll's waist was a sash of lilac silk, splitting into streamers. At the waist from the sash hung a little lilac bag, and inside was something hard, as Miranda pinched it.

'Oh, Miranda, let me look,' squealed Judy, holding out her hands for the discovery.

She grasped the doll and raced to her mother.

'Mother! Mother! Look what Miranda found, in a box under the floor,' she cried.

'It must have belonged to one of my great aunts,' pondered her mother, looking closely at the doll, examining the long drawers and the petticoat.

'What's in the pocket?' cried Judy, and she untied the little bag, and took out a silver groat dated 1836, and a minute pocket handkerchief edged with tiny lace.

'Oh, Judy. How lovely,' said her mother. 'I'll wash the dress and make a new sash and you can have your great-great-aunt's doll for your very own. She must have loved it. I wonder why she put it under the floor.'

'Perhaps she was going away,' said Judy.

'Perhaps she didn't put it there herself, but someone hid it and forgot it. Perhaps she died and the doll was forgotten,' said Mother sadly.

'I'll take the doll to bed with me and comfort her,' said Judy, and she kissed the faded little face, and stroked the doll.

That night the doll lay in Judy's arms in bed; it was kissed and comforted and sung to, but it seemed restless. It was not possible, of course, but Judy felt it move by itself. She took it out and laid it on the oak table by the bed, on a shawl for warmth.

'Lie there,' she whispered, and she stretched out her hand and touched the little figure in the darkness. Then she fell asleep, and she dreamed and dreamed of the doll. She was awakened suddenly by a slight sound, a little thud, and when she put out her fingers the doll had fallen to the carpet. She leaned over to pick it up, but the shawl was empty. The doll was walking stiffly on its little painted boots, and a shining light seemed to come from it, a halo surrounded the little creature. The light came not from the doll but from a child's hand which held it and guided its feet across the room. As Judy stared she could see the dim outline of a child in a long white nightdress gliding along the carpet, holding the doll's hand.

'Oh, my baby! I've got thee again. I've found thee, my love, my sweeting,' whispered a tiny voice soft as a dream, and the wind howled outside and thumped at the window and the owl in the fir tree hooted and called.

'Husha-by, my baby. Hush thee, my dear one,' crooned the little voice, and then it began to sing a lullaby.

Judy sat up in bed, shivering with excitement, half with fear and half with joy, for she could hear the tiny thuds of the doll's wooden feet pattering over the carpet, and see the faint light which went by the doll, outlining the shape of the little girl who led her away.

Then the doll disappeared, the light faded, and there was silence, except for the faint voice in the distance sighing, 'Oh, my dear one. Oh, my sweeting. I've found thee and we will never be parted again.'

Sighing with happiness which flooded the room and made her heart beat wildly, her mind singing like the little ghostie's voice, Judy fell asleep. Had she been dreaming, she wondered next day? The empty shawl lay on the floor, the doll had gone.

'The wee ghostie took back her doll last night,' she told her mother. 'She came for it and took it away. Oh, she was so glad, and I was glad too. I saw her, Mummy, in her white nightgown.'

'So that is what the poor little thing wanted,' said Judy's mother. 'She has been hunting for a hundred years or more, and now she has found her

treasure. I'm so happy about her. She won't come back any more, Judy. She will sleep now.'

But the mother was wrong. Judy saw her once again, walking across the room with her doll clasped in her arms, and her face smiling. Then, swinging the little wooden doll, dandling it gently, the ghostie faded and all was silent.

This story is by Alison Uttley.

A POCKETFUL OF STORIES FOR
FIVE YEAR OLDS
Collected by PAT THOMSON
Illustrated by Penny Dann

Put your hand into this pocketful of stories and you
will find . . . a giant with a terrible temper, shoes
that walk on their own at night, a little rabbit who
tells riddles, an owl who finds two strange bumps in
his bed, a busy headmaster whose wish comes true
. . . and many other funny and exciting people and
animals. you won't want to stop reading until you
get right to the bottom of the pocket!

Read Alone or Read Aloud

0 552 527181

**A BASKET OF STORIES FOR
SEVEN YEAR OLDS**
Collected by PAT THOMSON
Illustrated by Rachel Birkett

Climb into this basket of stories and you will find
. . . Charlie and his puppy, a wolf that tells riddles, a
witch, a smelly giant, and many other strange and
exciting people and animals. You won't want to stop
reading until you get right to the bottom of the
basket!

'Jam-packed with goodies' *The Sunday Telegraph*

'Will be enjoyed by children of all ages'
The Times Educational Supplement

'Will stimulate even the most reluctant reader'
Junior Education

Read Alone or Read Aloud

0 552 527297

A SACKFUL OF STORIES FOR
EIGHT YEAR OLDS
Collected by PAT THOMSON
Illustrated by Paddy Mounter

Delve into this sack of stories and you will find . . . a
Martian wearing Granny's jumper, that well-known
comic fairy-tale pair Handsel and Gristle, a unicorn,
a leprechaun, a princess who is a pig, and many other
strange and exciting characters. You won't want to
stop reading until you get right to the bottom of the
sack!

'There are thirteen stories to a sackful and each and
every one is a tried-and-tested cracker'
The Sunday Telegraph

'Will be enjoyed by children of all ages'
The Times Educational Supplement

'Will stimulate even the most reluctant reader'
Junior Education

Read Alone or Read Aloud

0 552 527300